# Celtic Irish Arousals

# Celtic Irish Arousals

## Short Stories

KIERON PINARD-BYRNE

# CELTIC IRISH AROUSALS
## SHORT STORIES

iUniverse books may be ordered through booksellers or by contacting:

iUniverse
1663 Liberty Drive
Bloomington, IN 47403
www.iuniverse.com
1-800-Authors (1-800-288-4677)

ISBN: 978-1-5320-8651-9 (sc)
ISBN: 978-1-5320-8650-2 (hc)
ISBN: 978-1-5320-8652-6 (e)

Library of Congress Control Number: 2019917319

Print information available on the last page.

iUniverse rev. date: 11/08/2019

This book is dedicated to

my wife, Kathleen;
my daughters, Jessica and Síle;
my sister, Celine;
me mammy, Josephine;

and all my other clan goddesses too numerous to mention who have nourished my life in mind, body, and spirit from my cradle to my delivery room.

May the protection of our ancestors be with us.
May they never quit.

# Contents

Backstabbers and Backstops ..................................................... 1

Outlook .................................................................... 11

Housekeepers .............................................................. 19

Staying the Course ........................................................ 27

Ireland's Eye .............................................................. 33

Andropause Wake .......................................................... 41

The Namesake ............................................................. 47

The Headhunt ............................................................. 53

Mother's Wake ............................................................. 61

The Well .................................................................. 67

Rose Vale ................................................................. 73

Walking on Air ............................................................ 79

Celibate Affairs ........................................................... 83

Mystique in Mustique ...................................................... 89

Kilcraic's Sixty-Three ...................................................... 97

The Kowtow ............................................................. 101

Golfer in the Rye .......................................................... 109

Epilogue: Betwixt and Between .............................................. 117

# Backstabbers and Backstops

Patrick J. O'Hara was in a reflective mood. After having put the finishing touches to his budget address, it was time to go home and spend the evening (or what was left of it) with his family. The hope of an inspirational fiscal fix to put the budget on a par with his previous ones, which had brought him acclaim as a preeminent finance minister, had kept him at his desk. It was now 7 p.m., and the workers' exodus from the city would be tailing off. It was time to go. He would accept the budget as a realistic one having regard for the economic climate of the hard times, and he'd face the inevitable furore that would be launched from the opposition benches when he delivered it. He was tempted to ignore the ringing phone and get the hell home whilst the moment of rationalisation was upon him, but his political astuteness had taught him never to turn his back on anything. It could be another opportunity knocking or a game changer.

"Hello?"

"Paddy?"

"Yeah."

"Connor."

"Who?"

"Connor Duffy."

"You haven't blown yourself up yet, then?"

"Paddy, you're in big trouble. We must meet immediately! We can't talk about it on the phone."

O'Hara was disturbed but adopted an offhand approach. "I can't be seen talking to the IRA."

"Talk to an old school chum, then. Believe you me, it is dynamite."

"OK, can you make Grafton Street entrance to the Green in thirty minutes or so?"

"I think so."

"I'll walk out and then back in. You follow, and when we're alone, we'll talk. OK?"

"OK."

O'Hara knew St Stephens Green would be relatively empty, and because it was raining, he could use his cap and umbrella to mask his identity. He put away his budget speech and called his secretary on the intercom. "You can leave now, but on your way out, tell Joe to have the Merc ready to move in one hour."

As soon as he heard his secretary leave, he put his overcoat on and calmly departed the building with a nod to the night guards. His mind was now finally off the budget. What was so damn important that a schoolmate, whom he had not seen in God knows how many years, should suddenly ring him up? What was the big trouble he was in? Was it risky to associate in this way with a known IRA man? He knew he could deal with that if by chance the press heard of the meeting. He hoped they wouldn't.

He was now in St Stephens Green, and as he'd expected, it was quite deserted. But for the rain and the nagging uncertainty, he would enjoy the stroll from the Earlsfort Terrace gate to the Grafton Street gate. The steps behind him had gone unnoticed until they had quickened and closed the distance between him and them. His head had only just begun to turn when he felt the deep pain of the blow struck to his lower back. "Bleeding Republican bastard!" he heard grunted in an unmistakable Northern accent. The first blow was followed by a barrage of fists struck at his head and ribcage as his arms were pulled behind him by a second assailant, who remorselessly kneed him. The mugging seemed to last an eternity. The pain, though excruciating, took second place as he struggled to get to his feet before someone found him and the press had a field day. He managed to stand up and staggered on wobbling legs back to his ministry building, where he saw the state car parked at the main door with its engine running. He collapsed into the back seat, and the car sped off.

From the moment he reached home, his wife, Doreen, took complete charge. His doctor diagnosed three broken ribs and a possible mild concussion. Before the ambulance arrived, Doreen had prepared his doctor's approved press release. "P. J. O'Hara fell when his horse suddenly bolted on the gallops, and he luckily escaped with only three broken ribs. He is a very resilient man and will be back at his desk after a short convalescence."

On admission to hospital, O'Hara was also diagnosed to have a fractured collarbone. Distressed though his injuries made him, they paled beneath the headlines of the morning press.

O'Hara Implicated in Illegal Gun-Running
Charges—Resignation Imminent

The thought that his political career was now being flushed into the Liffey overwhelmed his whole being. But for his incapacitation, he knew he could weather the storm. However, for the time being he would have to leave his political fate in the hands of the Taoiseach.

He guessed whoever had set him up on the gun-running charge had been behind the attack of the previous night. Presumably, the intention had been to restrict him to a hospital bed whilst his political assassination took place. He provisionally decided subject to discussion with the Taoiseach to call in the Special Branch. Their starting point would be Connor Duffy, if he could be found. With this trend of planning, he was completely unprepared for the Taoiseach, who arrived unannounced at his bedside.

The Taoiseach, not generally known as a cold-blooded type, adopted an uncompromising stance for the first time in his political life. "I want your resignation."

O'Hara, a known cool and calculating politician who met every situation as though he were prepared for it, responded abruptly, "You'll have to sack me."

"I'll give you till 6 p.m. to resign. If not, I'll sack you."

"You don't have to do anything you don't want to."

"I have a report from the Guarda Commissioner. The leader of the opposition has the same report. The British government is fully in the loop. There's no other way, and I won't stand idly by."

"Do you believe a scintilla of the British bull?" O'Hara asked.

"There are copies of all the incriminating intelligence in this file, which I'll leave with you. When you read it, you'll see that you have no option but to resign."

"Do you still have the balls to ask me how I am?"

"How are you, Paddy?"

O'Hara's statement, prepared by his solicitor for the six o'clock news, said he was completely innocent of the alleged illegal gun-running charges. The nine o'clock news included a statement from the government information service that P. J. O'Hara had been dismissed as finance minister.

Patrick J. O'Hara's ascendancy to political preeminence had been so successful that defeat was not part of his vocabulary. His humiliating sacking had changed that. The ambition which he had diligently worked to attain from the time of his first election to D'fhail Eireann suddenly evaporated. How could he ever be Taoiseach? If not, the plans of his select political coterie would not be fulfilled. What would his supporters be thinking tonight of his sudden change of fortune? It'd been fifty-plus years since the Easter uprising, and they (like he) had seen the reality of what was happening in twenty-six county politics. The political will to achieve a united Ireland was rapidly being eroded. The populist urgency was with the economy and their materialism. The new political generation and classes usurped by self-greed had very little time for the aspirations of their rebel ancestors, who had delivered Ireland into partitioned nationhood. By the turn of the century, who would be left to drive the British out?

P. J. O'Hara's supporters were attuned to the urgent demands from the graves of every Irish martyr—that a steely eyed leader must come forward now and fulfil the desire of their immortal souls. He was seen as that leader, one who could satisfy a unanimous mandate for economic prosperity due to his track record in all the ministries he had commanded. He would also be a leader with an unswerving devotion to uniting Ireland by the only possible successful means of forcing a British withdrawal engineered with American funding and diplomatic gurus. Plans had been well advanced for his takeover as party leader. A majority of party TDs had already pledged their support to him, and it only remained for him to choose the moment of his succession. That night he had agonised over not having brought the showdown with the incumbent party leader and the Taoiseach to a finale. It crossed his mind that perhaps his enemies from within had set him up to avoid that pivotal showdown. If so, it was the final proof that a mindset averse to a united Ireland in the body politic was more rampant than he and his coterie understood.

The fruits of P. J. O'Hara's wedlock to a former Taoiseach's daughter could not be gainsaid. Doreen was indeed the quintessential woman behind his greatness. He valued her political insights and knack for getting to the nub of any issue. In marriage they had become Ireland's power couple, as famous as its forty shades of green. But pondering upon these pluses in his life would not, he knew, solve the mighty political conflagration he must overcome before he could reach his pinnacle.

Doreen's arrival at his bedside brought him relief from his gloom. Her news lit him up. "The telegrams are pouring in from all over the country, and they're all saying the same thing more or less: 'Hang in there, Paddy. We are with you all the way.' The phone hasn't stopped ringing; I've taken many of the calls myself. I swear to God, Paddy, your people are with you 100 per cent. They expect you to fight this thing. I expect you to fight, and our children know you will."

"Bejesus, Doreen, it looks like the traitors intend to put me on trial on these gun-running charges. If they do, chances are they must have enough evidence to put me away. If they do, that's it. The game is up."

"If they go to court, it will be a jury case. What twelve Dublin jurors will find Paddy O'Hara guilty of running guns into the North to stop the slaughter of Irish Catholics?"

"You think I did it, then?" O'Hara asked his wife.

"Paddy, I don't know what you did or didn't do, but either way I'm with you, and either way you have to stand your ground."

"You're right. We've got a lot of catching up to do, but for now let's be clear on one thing: I am not guilty of any illegal gun running. I've been set up, and the sooner I get out of here and get the bastards responsible, the better."

"It will be a grand comeback: the case goes to trial, and you're found not guilty."

"Then I'll throw down the gauntlet."

Sleep would not come easy, and when it did, it was of short reprieve. During his waking hours, O'Hara consoled himself with the belief his power and his grassroots support was still intact. If he could win in court, there was still a chance he could realise his ambition to attain absolute power and use it as it must be used—to get reunification.

He was asleep and shouting "Traitors" when the night nurse tenderly cupped his face.

"Are you all right, Mr O'Hara?" she said.

"Yes, yes. I guess I was having a nightmare."

"It's a terrible thing they are doing to you, Mr O'Hara."

"What's that?"

"Sacking you for trying to help the poor Catholics in Derry defend themselves."

"Where are you from, then?"

"Sure aren't I from your very own constituency, Mr O'Hara."

"Is that so? And what might your name be?"

"Catherine O'Toole, but call me Cathy. All me friends do."

"Does that mean I'm your friend, then, Cathy?"

"Sure didn't I vote for you as soon as I turned 18. Me father says you're the only one with a head on his shoulders and fire in the belly. According to him, you should have been running the country a long time ago."

"You don't think that twelve good Dublin men like your father will find me guilty?"

"Indeed I don't. They'll make a hero out of you, Mr O'Hara. I've got to be going now to do me rounds. I'll look in on you again before morning, but if you need me for anything, just press the buzzer."

## *Thirteen Years Later*

The television cameras of the world were on Taoiseach Patrick J. O'Hara. No Irish men or women were in their armchairs or kitchens, or so it seemed from the heads that filled every inch of O'Connell Street and beyond. Those who could not see O'Hara would hear him over the hundreds of loudspeakers perched in every Dublin city street.

It seemed God and St Patrick were there that fateful day because the rain clouds had disappeared into clear, heavenly skies of glorious sunlight. Every Irish martyr was there for the last hurrah: the names of Emmet, Tone, Pearse, Collins, and company were held aloft, emblazoned on emerald banners, their names chanted and echoed. The songs of Ireland were sung over and over to the accompaniment of heart-thumping music.

On 24 April 1916, Patrick Pearse had delivered the Irish proclamation at Dublin's general post office. Now, on that hallowed ground, Patrick J. O'Hara stood tall. Ireland was again moving inexorably towards the fulfilment of Pearse's proclaimed vision following the British government's declared intent to withdraw from Northern Ireland. P. J. O'Hara's historic moment to copper-fasten Pearse's legacy had arrived. His voice rang out.

Irish men and Irish women at home and abroad, it is with profound joy we celebrate today the agreement brokered between the sovereign governments of Britain and Ireland. Within ten years, this great country of ours will be reunited. Wherever you are today, be in Ireland then. Come home to an all-Ireland republic. The land our forefathers fought for time and again, shed their blood for, and died for is truly ours to enjoy and develop, and we will live in prosperity. Together, we will make it "A Nation Once Again."

The church bells commenced ringing with the spontaneous, euphoric shouts and applause of the gathered people. From the gathering, a single gunshot was audible. As P. J. O'Hara lay mortally wounded on the steps of the GPO, pandemonium erupted on O'Connell Street. Two hours later, Patrick J. O'Hara's death was announced to the world.

With North and South Ireland plunged into states of emergency, the British government revoked its intent to withdraw from Northern Ireland, the termination of Ireland's partition backstops laid low in smithereens.

# Outlook

A breakfast coddle was on the stove. Dolly and Mixture, the black and white rat catchers housed in the basement, had been milked and fed again. Plants, cut flowers, box plants, lettuces, and cabbages were on their pedestals out front. It was 6 a.m., and the Nut Grove was open as usual. Its proprietor, Stephen J. Byrne, was known all over Dublin by his signature headdress as Straw Hat. Twenty years before, they called him Jazzer in the docklands and flour mills, until he realised his dream and became a green grocer.

A parade of night workers, dockers, and postal sorters arrived first for their Player's Please, Sweet Afton, Carrols No. 1, or Woodbine Cigarettes, as well as granny smiths—an apple a day keeps the doctor away. Flattery and "See you on the telly tonight" replaced the usual rush of banter and blarney. But Skipper as always hung about for a chat because he had only to cross the road to commence postal sorting supervision duties at 7 a.m.

"So how's the form today, Skipper? Are you glad you're not sorry?" wooed Straw Hat.

"Sure, I can't wait for the summer and our annual scout camp. Your boys must get the crew cut this year for that."

"'Tis a great job you're doing for my two. We didn't have the choices you're giving them. Sure in my day, we didn't even have shoes to wear running about!"

"Are you all set for your address to the nation tonight? Sure after that, they'll want to put you in the Mansion House. Lord Mayor of Dublin, no less!"

"Go to God, 'tis pulling me leg, you are! You're a grand one for the blarney!"

"I'll be watching and praying for inspiration," said Skipper, giving the three-finger scout salute as he departed.

Mrs Early was living out her end times filled with a quiet misery and despair in rooms across the street from the Nut Grove. Though her spirit was kind and gentle, her presence and name reminded him of Biddy Early tales of the occult in western Ireland. Her all-black attire and dark features invited such feelings.

"How are you today, Mrs Early?" said Straw Hat as she entered the shop.

"Didn't get a wink's sleep all night, what with the arthritis and all playing up; the pain was something terrible. But I can't complain too much. Sure poor Mrs Galvin is all backed up again with the constipation and what have you. I'll take a few spuds, a head of cabbage, and two bottles of milk. And if you don't mind, put them in the book till I collect the pension at the end of the week!"

"If I were a head of cabbage, I'd cut myself in two. The leaves I'd give to many, but the heart I'd give to you," said Straw Hat, hoping to cheer Mrs Early up.

"Oh, go on now, out of that. Who'd be wantin' an old fecking fart like me?"

"These days, sure you never know your luck. Anyways, I went

into the garden this morning and cut this lovely bunch of dahlias for your mantelpiece!"

"Aren't you the holy terror for thinking of me? And all you have to think about, what with going on the telly tonight, and won't I be watching you in Belton's Pub with me glass of Guinness," said Mrs Early as she departed, clutching the flowers to her flagging breasts with one hand and lugging her bag of shopping with the other.

Rita, an elder spinster sister of his wife, was the only shop assistant after his eldest daughter up and married the Nut Grove's horticultural supplier and a great tenor of the "Wild Colonial Boy" to boot. Rita arrived for work daily by train to the Amiens Street train station every morning at eight and departed the shop at 5 p.m. She was not long for this life, having been diagnosed with a brain tumour as the cause of her excruciating headaches and her generally being a Mrs Difficulty. Plans were afoot for her to take over the running of Straw Hat's home whilst his wife had agreed to take up Rita's job in the shop. He longed for that day to come as he watched Rita slicing cheese and being Mrs Difficulty again with a customer. Rather than upset her with a rebuke, he slipped out to go next door and visit Mrs Galvin.

The Galvin sisters had come up from the country many moons ago to meet some jackeens they had met at the Galway races. When their dalliances didn't work out, they stayed on in Dublin and eventually opened a store next door to the Nut Grove, with a tea parlour to service the culchies who came up to Dublin for shopping or football matches. But after the younger Galvin sister died suddenly in their living quarters above, the store business went downhill, and nowadays the store was more often closed than open.

"There you are, Mrs Galvin, and there's a Turkish delight to cheer you up!" said Straw Hat after knocking and entering her sitting room.

"Well, go on now, and do your Yeats impersonation. Sure it will do me a world of good as it always does."

"I will bedad," said Straw Hat, and he proceeded to recite Yeats's "Down by the Sally Gardens" with gusto.

Down by the Sally gardens my love and I did meet; she passed the Sally gardens with little snow white feet. She bid me take love easy, as the leaves grow on the tree; but I being young and foolish with her did not agree.

In a field by the river my love and I did stand, and on my leaning shoulder she laid her snow white hand; she bid me take life easy as the grass grows on the weirs; but I was young and foolish and now I'm full of tears.

"Isn't that the be all and end all of it?" replied a heartily clapping Mrs Galvin.

"Anyways, Mrs Early says you're not up to the mark, so I passed in," Straw Hat said as the clapping petered out.

"Ah, sure I don't know whether I'm coming or going these days. The last time I had to go into Jervis Street hospital, they stuck pellets up me back passage. I'll not go through that humiliation again," replied a flushed Mrs Galvin.

Straw Hat relieved the embarrassing admission with his tried and trusted prescription. "Well, I left some overripe bananas, which won't sell, on the table. Believe you me, if you take them for your supper tonight, you'll be right as rain come the morning—if not before!"

"Me mammy only ever did promise me I'd be better before I'm twice married, and see where that got me. Anyways, I'll be staying up for your pep talk tonight; sure that can't do me any harm," concluded Mrs Galvin, blowing kisses as Straw Hat took his leave.

The Nut Grove's morning trade of commerce and social

intercourse with the neighbourhood housewives was brisk as ever and full of gossip. Poor Lizzy O'Toole had been stood up outside the picture house and molested on her way home by a Northumberland street gang. There had been a shindig in Belton's pub, and the Gardaí had been called in to restore order. Mrs O'Dea's husband had gone home plastered drunk and beat her black and blue again. Kilmartins turf accountants had been broken into, but as the day's takings had been banked, the robbers got nothing. And "that rip Delores O'Hara had run off to England with a bun in the oven."

Three doors up from the Nut Grove was the Cafollas' fish and chip shop, which Mario, an immigrant from Italy, had opened to great neighbourhood fanfare back in the good old days. It was deserted when Straw Hat entered, and upon seeing Mario glum behind the counter, Straw Hat recited his favourite riddle. "I was walking over the Butt Bridge with me breakfast under me arm. A man fired a shot at me. It passed right through me, and it hit a man behind me, but it never touched me!"

"Jesus be praised, me mickey be raised, aren't you a sight for sore eyes. I thought you'd be home shampooing yourself for tonight's performance," was Mario's rhetorical reply.

"No need for that when the best way to a man's heart is through his stomach with a good feed of fish and chips covered with lots of salty vinegar," said Straw Hat to end their standoff and order his lunch.

Whilst Mario prepared Straw Hat's lunch, they consoled each other on their declining business due to the movement of people out to Dublin Corporation's new housing schemes in the suburbs, and they swore to continue to keep each other's spirits up come hail, rain, snow, or sunshine.

The day's routine of serving customer needs, consoling the hardship stories of this one and that one, cajoling with others, or taking time out to water the plants, flowers, and vegetables continued after lunch until six o'clock and the call to prayer, when the angelus rang out from the bells of the Pro Cathedral over Dublin.

Father Mee rang up Straw Hat from Belcamp College at three o'clock. It was a pet prank of this holy father to inquire of others as to what they might be doing at the hour they crucified Christ. The Nut Grove had a barter arrangement with Belcamp College to exchange sacks of coal for Queens potatoes and free-range eggs. On barter days, Straw Hat dined with the seminary's great teachers over piping-hot Irish stew. He loved this weekly ritual and the drive into the countryside with the wind whipping through his van, and on the way back he'd visit his daughter's family and farm. They concluded their barter deal with agreement in principle on quantities for Straw Hat's upcoming visit.

A Mr Houlihan arrived for a marriage consultation just as Rita was going off shift. Mr Houlihan, who had "six lovely lassies", had lost his wife to cancer and had been seeing a spinster ten years his junior for the past year. She now wanted the ring on her finger to become Mrs Houlihan. Straw Hat had also lost his first wife to cancer. The difference in experience between them was that he only had two lovely daughters at the time of bereavement but now had another sweetheart daughter and five sons with his second wife. For these reasons, Straw Hat had been recommended to Mr Houlihan as the best man to point him in the right direction. After a lot of soul searching over a pot of tea and a mutual recognition that life was for the living—one simply had to make the most of it because one was only passing through—an elated Mr Houlihan departed for his home to explain to his daughters that they were going to have a stepmother to help in their rearing.

The Nut Grove opened for business six days a week from dawn to around midnight. The late hours were to serve night shift workers and to catch the neighbours on their way home from the pubs. Tonight was different. Straw Hat had to close at ten to shave and put on a change of clothes in preparation for his TV appearance.

At 10.30 p.m. sharp, a limousine arrived and parked outside. The chauffeur alighted and stood in readiness to open the back door for him. Straw Hat came out transformed. A trilby replaced his straw hat, a maroon bow tie replaced the brown and white polka dot one over a freshly starched stud collar, a double-breasted charcoal grey suit replaced his shop coat and dungarees, and Clarks patent leather shoes replaced his boots. He saw McHugh himself three doors down outside his bicycle repair shop giving him the thumbs-up. Mrs Early then whisked past him as if on a broom, headed for the pub on the corner, and she said, "May the Holy Ghost be with you." Outside the pub, a crowd had gathered to witness the spectacle; Mario was at his door with a big smile on his face. As Straw Hat entered the limousine, he looked up and saw Mrs Galvin wave from her bedroom window. He felt like Jazzer Byrne walking on air again.

The limousine drove up Amiens Street, up Talbot Street, onto O'Connell Street, across O'Connell Bridge, around College Green, and up Dame Street. Then it headed south for Donnybrook and the television studios of Radio Telefis Eireann. He had not experienced such travelling grandeur in Dublin before, but he would do so again on the way back because the limousine was to return him to the Nut Grove from where he would drive home in his van.

When he was shown into the recording studio, Father Burke, the resident theologian of Belcamp College, was deep in discussion with production staff. Straw Hat thanked his chaperone and announced himself. "I am from the University of Adversity. The last time I was here, I was a Seagull."

Father Burke then formally introduced him to the amused staff. "This is the man I told you all about, the man with the great knack of explaining the great mysteries of our religion, the one and only Stephen J. Byrne."

*Outlook* was the name of Father Burke's nightly five-minute TV sermon, which was broadcast live after the late news at 11.30 p.m. For four minutes and thirty seconds, they discussed Thomas á Kempis's classic book *The Imitation of Christ*, the theology surrounding the eye of a needle and a mustard seed, and humans' need for transcendence. Father Burke then faced the camera and said, "Well, that's it for tonight's *Outlook*. Any final words, Stephen?"

"Do you see this pencil?" He held it up. "Do you see this empty sheet of paper?" He held it up too. "Well, like this pencil and paper, I would have no words to say if it were not for the love of our Lord, Jesus Christ."

# Housekeepers

On the third Sunday of every month, if not in Lourdes, Fatima, Lough Derg, or Knock, and if not ill or snowed in, May Redmond took the bus from Delgany to Dublin. By O'Connell Bridge, she would meet up with her lifelong friend Eileen, and together they bussed from Dublin to Raheny to visit with May's married sister Josie. Having worked as housekeeper to the aristocracy all her adult life, May was now a plump, matronly, healthy 60-year-old ready to be put out to pasture by her employer in July. One year before, her 90-year-old father had provided the accommodation for her twilight years with a gift inter vivos of his family home to her and his only other spinster daughter, who had died suddenly soon after the property transferred. Since then, May had been trying to come to terms with the prospect of moving back in alone with her daddy and looking after him whilst dealing with her own fears of cronehood followed by haghood. That was until Alec's letter arrived on Friday and provided her with an unexpected alternative.

Eileen was also a 60-year-old spinster but of slighter girth and with a heart murmur. Otherwise, she and May were as Siamese twins, having shared a life outside housekeeping services on holidays and monthly visits to Josie. She was constantly remonstrating with herself and fretting as to how she may live out her remaining years on her meagre savings and pension. Following the untimely death of May's joint legatee, she became determined to convince May to let her lodge with her and her father. She planned to put her request to May and expected Josie would be in full support.

In preparation for the 4.30 p.m. arrival of May and Eileen, Josie was busy in the kitchen as usual. The table was set. The salad, comprising of freshly picked lettuce and scallions from the garden with lots of hard-boiled eggs, was ready. Apple and rhubarb tarts were baking in the oven. These delicacies would be supplemented with May's Russian log and Eileen's marble cake, both from the Kylemore bakery. Meanwhile, there were lots of cheese and ham sandwiches to be made and turnover breads to be sliced and buttered for pairing with a selection of jams.

Josie was an attractive middle-aged mother with slate-blue, pleading eyes below a shock of wavy grey hair. The demands of housekeeping for a large family were beginning to take their toll on her health. Apart from her daily visits to the shops and the butcher, she had become virtually housebound in looking after her husband and six children. Nevertheless, she also enjoyed catering to her regular visitors from her large, extended, chatty family.

As Josie waited for the hall doorbell to chime, she went over in her mind the good news she had for May. The widow of their youngest brother, who had been lodging for donkey's years with and housekeeping for their father, had been offered a house from the Dublin Corporation for herself and her three daughters and son, and all of them would be out of their father's hair by July. May could move in as planned and start looking after their father, which he was much looking forward to.

Following the usual greetings ritual in the hallway—the disrobing of hats, scarves, overcoats, and umbrellas onto the hall stand—May asked that the three of them retire into the sitting room because she had some "interesting news" to share. With Josie and Eileen seated on the sofa, May presented them with the "totally unexpected letter" she had received on Friday and suggested that they read it together whilst she went upstairs to powder her nose.

4 Willow Oaks Road
Lee-on-Solent
England
17 March 1961

My Dear May,

Since my beloved wife departed this life, I have been weary with sorrow and trepidation for my future. By my doctor's advice, all things being equal, I have a good ten to fifteen years ahead of me. But what to do?

My son wishes me to sell my home and move in with him. I am not, however, disposed to having his wife and children rule my roost. As an alternative, he suggested I sell my home and move into an old folks' retirement home. Again, not a very inviting way to recoil for an old navy man like me.

To cut a long saga short, I have been inspired to request your hand in marriage. Given my animus, I hasten to add we shall of course enjoy immunity from conjugal rights. Ours would be a platonic marital relationship of respectful friendship. My wife, as you know, was very fond of you and Eileen, and I know she would approve. So over to you, dear May. I would leave all the planning and details in your capable hands. Living in hope of your favourable reply.

Kindest regards,
Alec

Eileen sat deflated with renewed feelings of being left on the shelf again. After all, if Alec had chosen her, all her retirement challenges would be resolved. Now, if May up and married Alec, even her hopes to lodge with May and her father would be dashed.

Josie, on the other hand, relaxed, chuffed in her favourite armchair. After years of housekeeping for her parents and caring for her dying mother, she had blossomed late by marriage to a widower.

Eileen blurted out, "I am infuriated by May's connivances. Her father's plans to be looked after are now in tatters after he went and gave her his house. What a feckless rip!"

When May returned from the powder room, she thought Eileen looked as if she had seen a ghost. Eileen sat smouldering. Josie quickly rescued the trio from the awkwardness of the moment by announcing, "Well, May, if you want to go ahead with this, I'll look after me daddy; he can move in here."

Not to be outdone, Eileen offered to be an ex gratia live-in housekeeper for their father if May wanted to accept Alec's proposal. May responded enthusiastically to Josie's announcement, stating Josie was in fact the best one to look after their father; in any case, money would not be a problem because when she sold the house, she would be sending cash monthly to cover Josie's extra costs. With these undertakings agreed, they chatted on, planning for a July wedding, until it was time for Josie to put the kettle on for high tea.

Alec had been less mortified since posting his letter to May. His feelings of mortification until then were but a condition of his entrapment in misery since his wife had departed. The growth of the bags below his eyes were a testimony to his misery: he had not been sleeping well or coping well with being alone and the daily grind of self-catering. He had been longing for the good old days of being in the navy without a care in the world. Now, even to shave and bathe had become a chore because such daily rituals were a constant reminder of his seventy-year-old body and his mortality. Even his nightly ritual of a pint of bitters and a single red breast at his local pub brought no relief to his constant confrontations with melancholy. When the solution presented itself to him one evening, he was momentarily infatuated by the possibilities. Then he quickly ruled out all the likely lonely English roses with whom he might risk taking such a leap of faith or adventure. Then his wife's friends May and Eileen crossed his mind. The next morning, he busied himself with varying drafts of a letter that would not reveal him to be "a silly old codger". Three days later, he finally signed and sealed his umpteenth version of his letter to May, managed a shave without nicks, and walked (briskly, for a change) to the postbox in Lee-on-Solent.

After the mailing, he adopted a regimen of positive thinking. His chemist recommended an iron tonic. That with daily morning and evening walks along the shore, and a good dinner out every night at six, served to return his vigour and zest for life. Then the alchemy of May's letter restored his bliss.

The Great House
Delgany
Co Wicklow
Ireland

24 March 1961

My Dear Alec,

'Tis a wise man of three score and ten years who can choose to do what is best for him and in the firm knowledge that his dearly beloved deceased wife would approve. I am therefore pleased to accept your kind proposal of matrimony.

I have discussed plans with my sister Josie for us to be married in St Brigid's Church, Killester, in July and for her to host a small family reception at her home following. On your receipt of this letter, we can agree all the necessary arrangements over the phone.

I do hope this finds you well and will put an end to your worrying. Rest assured when I start looking after you as your wife, you will have nothing to worry about.

Yours very truly,
May

*Twenty-Five Years Later*

Alec, as expected by his GP, lived out another blissful fifteen years of retirement after his marriage to May. As if that was not good enough for him, he also had the good fortune to pass away in his sleep. May soldiered on all alone with her birthright of longevity, always the good housekeeper, until her heart gave out on a cold winter's morning in her hallway. As she lay akimbo on the cold grey floor tiles, she asked her God for forgiveness. She had never forgiven herself for not sharing the kitty from her father's house with Josie. The cash had been deposited to her bank account four weeks after she'd become ensconced with Alec in Lee-on-Solent. On second thoughts, she decided to hold on to this nest egg until she was sure her marriage to Alec proved hospitable. When that hurdle had been crossed and she was fully in charge, she had nourished the need to keep hording it for a rainy day, just in case she needed it after Alec passed on. That need never materialised because Alec left her well heeled, but it was replaced by the need, as she aged further, to never run out of money. In any case, she always knew things had worked out perfectly well for her daddy. Under Josie's tender loving care, he had lived to the ripe old age of 100. And so May had been moved to change her will and leave the kitty to the cats home in Portsmouth and all the rest, residue, and remainder of her estate to five Celtic Twilight literary movements in equal shares, whose authors' books had kept her sane in her widowhood.

# Staying the Course

*In memory of John Redmond (1873–1973)*

Jacob was now of the age of his grandfather when he entered the home stretch. Like an owl, he was bright-eyed, symbolic of the goddess Athena who knew at a glance. She was the goddess of wisdom, learning, and augury. In regression, he was an altar boy, a boy scout, and a budding student of life.

On deathblow day, he was the only one home alone with his mammy when the big black telephone on the hall stand rang. When she hung up, she explained, ashen faced, how her 48-year-old brother, Uncle Jack, had had a massive heart attack whilst having lunch with his family. He had been rushed to Jervis Street Hospital by ambulance only to be pronounced dead on arrival. Because Jack's wife was too bereaved to look after Jack's 90-year-old father, Jacob's mammy had to have Jacob cycle over to Donneycarney and bring his grandfather home on the bus.

With the bus fare for his grandfather stashed safely away in his corduroys' secret pocket, Jacob set out on his Mary Hannigan bicycle to chaperone his grandfather. When he opened the front gate to his grandfather's home, the front door opened too. Without ado, his grandfather was coldly passed out. They walked sprightly down Collins Avenue to the bus stop, his grandfather carrying an overnight bag and Jacob wheeling Mary Hannigan's bicycle. At the bus stop, their silence continued in waiting. When the bus arrived, Jacob handed the fare to the bus conductor and asked that his grandfather be let off at the fish and chipper in Harmonstown.

Jacob had never raced Mary Hannigan's bicycle since she had given it to him so he could cycle in reverence to St Bridget's Church, Killester, to serve Mass; she was sure he had received the calling to the priesthood just like her elder brother, Blackser. Jacob was only convinced, with all the stops the bus must make, that he should arrive before it, and by the skin of his teeth, he did. Reunited, Jacob and his grandfather walked silently across Harmonstown Bridge, which overlooked the train station, and went into Ennafort Park and home, where his mammy immediately put on the kettle for tea and had a long chat with her daddy.

Not long after his Uncle Jack's death, but after much family wheeling and dealing, his grandfather's home in Donneycarney was sold. Until then, his grandfather's daily rituals had kept him hale and hearty. Every night he retired between 11.30 and midnight to rise again by 10 a.m. for a light breakfast and to study the form. After lunch, he walked up Collins Avenue and spent the remains of the day between his local pub and bookie shop. At around 6 p.m., he walked down Collins Avenue, dined, and then relaxed till bedtime, smoking his pipe, reading the evening newspapers, and listening to the radio. That daily routine was broken only on the Sabbath, when he walked down Collins Avenue to attend midday Mass in Donneycarney Church and then walked up Collins Avenue to the pub for a few bottles of Guinness before lunch. His son-in-law would regularly pick him up at the pub and take him to his daughter's Sunday feast.

It was from these Sunday visits that Jacob learnt his grandfather was not a conversationalist but rather a wise old owl like the one in his father's frequent recitation:

> A wise old owl sat in an oak,
> The more he saw,
> The less he spoke,
> The less he spoke the more he heard,

Oh why can't we all be like that wise old owl?

When imprisoned in his new Ennafort Park home, Jacob's grandfather took a turn for the worse. He discontinued his daily walks because he had no desire to make new friends at his new neighbourhood bookie shop or pub. He could only keep in touch with his old friends when his son-in-law would take him on Sundays for a few bottles of Guinness at his old neighbourhood pub, Belton's on Collins Avenue. These lifestyle changes resulted in a weekday routine of watching horse racing, news, and miscellany on the telly in his snug armchair from 10 a.m. till midnight.

So that he could resume his horse racing hobby, his daughter and caregiver brought Jacob to meet the manageress of Killmartins bookie shop in Harmonstown, Miss Dellahunty. When his mammy explained to Miss Dellahunty how her father had been uprooted and become depressed, and how it would be great if she would allow his grandson to place his bets, Miss Dellahunty said she was sure that would not be a problem at all, adding, "Sure your son has a grand, mature presence and all the makings of a professional gambler about him." Miss Dellahunty then explained all that had to be done was for Jacob to bring his grandfather's betting slips and his bets to her window, and she would hand out tickets. If any ticket became a winning ticket, it should be brought back to her window, and she would hand over the winnings.

That year, Jacob's daddy had fixed him up with a summer job to learn the green grocery and horticultural retail trade at Dervin's in Killester, with a view in following summers for Jacob to work knowledgeably in his father's Nut Grove in Amiens Street. Cathy, Dervin's assistant, was charged with his training. But when it came time for Jacob to return to school, Cathy, to titillate him, gave him a gleaming picture of herself with the friendly advice that he should not chance wasting himself neither on the priesthood nor on the green grocery trade. Cathy's incorrigible chastisement and his accumulated wages prompted Jacob to follow Miss Dellahunty's insight and try his luck at becoming a professional gambler by understudying his grandfather.

Snotser was the resident professional gambler of Killmartins in Harmonstown. Every day, that bookie shop was always full of men like Snotser on the dole. They called him Snotser because when the results were coming in, he sweated from his nostrils. When Snotser saw Jacob was a regular visitor to the winning window, he befriended him to learn his system. Jacob's grandfather's system was simple. In the flat season, he bet a shilling to win on each of two carefully chosen Lester Pigott daily mounts. In the national hunt season, he bet a shilling to win on each of two Josh Gifford daily mounts provided they were trained by Captain Ryan Price. The only exceptions were when his grandfather wished to bet shillings on Tom Draper–trained horses provided they were ridden by Pat Taffe, but he would not bet on their Ann Duchess of Westminster's Arkle, who was the champion steeplechaser of all time and therefore always raced at unbeatable odds. Jacob's system was to simply double his grandfather's bets once he had experienced his grandfather's good luck. Snotser bragged he must increase his stake if he ever wanted to become rich, but Jacob remained loyal to his grandfather's approach. This meant he no longer depended upon his mother's supply of broadleaf cigarettes because he could afford his preferred brand of Rothmans and could fund his scouting hiking and camping outings.

For three years in being his grandfather's runner, their wheels of good fortune continued, whereupon with a nod and a wink, his grandfather handed him a ten-pound note and a betting slip which read, "Ten pounds, win—Reynard's Heir." Snotser jeered that Reynard's Heir, like Jacob's grandfather, was a silly old nag. He advised Jacob to pocket the ten pounds or bet it five pounds each way on Kathleen Rua. Jacob, not wishing to break faith with his grandfather, handed in the bet to Miss Dellahunty: twenty pounds to win, Reynard's Heir.

Wanting to be spared of Snotser's jeering when the result came in, Jacob ducked into Killmartins in Fairview as soon as he was released from school that afternoon. He was busying himself studying the day's racing results when he felt from behind a pair of hands tightening around his neck, followed by the voice of Redser, his Irish language school teacher.

"Since when does the juvenile Black Byrne dabble in the sport of kings?"

"My name is not Black Byrne, sir. 'Tis Jacob, and your name is Mr Martin, not Redser, sir."

"You're getting too big for your bleeding britches, you little prick! So tell me now, what town in Ireland spells the same front to back and back to front?"

"I just don't know, sir!"

"You stupid moron, 'tis staring you straight in the face on that race card. 'Tis Navan, you fecking fool."

Jacob, following that scolding, was forced to explain to Mr Martin that he was awaiting the next result from Navan because his grandfather had a flutter on Reynard's Heir, and it was his job to give his grandfather the result when he got home. Mr Martin agreed to grant Jacob absolution for breaking the law by being in a turf accountant's shop, but only after calling his grandfather a "feckless old fart wasting his old age pension on an old, worn-out piece of horseshit like Reynard's Heir." Triumphantly, a trio of old farts burst into an Irish jig with their ringleader, singing over and over again "Horses for Courses". This spectacle had been brought about by the clerk of the shop marking Reynard's Heir the twelve-to-one winner of the 3.30 p.m. race at Navan! When the old farts' celebration subsided, their ringleader informed all present that young or old, in going firm, going soft, going hard, or going yielding, Reynard's Heir from his cradle and now to his grave had never lost a race at Navan, though he had never won any place else. As Jacob left Killmartins, he also learnt that Mr Martin may not have inherited the nickname Redser for his red hair alone, but possibly for his red face when seized in uncontrollable anger.

That evening Jacob's grandfather, in the spirit of Guinness, revealed that being in the home stretch was like riding Arkle, galloping miraculously for the Gold Cup winning post, and that when he would ascend from that ley line, he was expecting great gas because he knew for sure Jesus's spiritual grandmother Aíne, canonised St Anna, was a revered Celtic princess, a Druid priestess, and a fine specimen for women throughout her life. In tandem, he jested in earnest blarney—and which Jacob, in living, learnt to be true—that the best philosophy in the human race is to be in this world but not of it, because otherwise the public lavatory philosophy dominates. "Remember, man, the job is never finished till the paperwork is done."

# Ireland's Eye

Family legend had it Fionn and Fergus were descendants of Brian Boru, the high king of Ireland, who in 1014 had changed the course of Viking Irish history at the Battle of Clontarf. Brian Boru won that battle but lost his life.

When they descended in youthful exuberance upon Clontarf that fateful August day, their spirits instinctively imbibed the energy of its hallowed land. They lived as soldiers of destiny within the spirit of their times, Fionn as a carpenter and Fergus as a born-again artist. Nixers provided the means for their pursuit of social happiness—dances, soccer, Guinness, and craic. By the time Fionn parked his car outside the Dollymount house address he had been given by his mentor, Fergus was in protest, bemoaning the waste of a glorious summer's day to be spent indoors. When the interior of the house roof they were there to replace snowed its dust upon them, they ran out of the house in glee, shaking the dust off themselves, laughing, spitting, and coughing. Then they sprawled out on the lush green lawn. This work interruption, until the dust had settled, provided them an unscheduled respite to engage in brotherly daydreaming of their lives to come. Fergus saw the roof collapse as an omen to end his nixer days, emigrate to California, and become an artistic legend of sorts. Fionn's oracle told him he must continue the hard grind of day work and night school, followed by full-time training in Gorey's Teacher Training College in Wexford, where he'd become the woodwork teacher of his aspirations; all of this was nourished by his teacher, mentor, and ultimately close friend.

In their youth, only eighteen months of lifetime separated them. But thirty years later, when Fionn was diagnosed with mesothelioma, the first known asbestos victim of an anticipated epidemic to come in Ireland, they had long been separated by emigration and the tug of their own families. Now they were separated more by the spirits of knowing and not knowing of their deaths to come. By this time, Fergus had become part bard, part ovate, and part Druid; he was a dabbler in esoteric arts of living. He was at the time of Fionn's death sentence moving in Mayan prophecy cult circles, enraptured by the prospects. The Age of the Fifth Sun was scheduled to end in 2012 with the destruction of the earth, similar to the disappearance of Atlantis. Alternatively, he understood a transitional regeneration to a New Age of the Sixth Sun would commence on earth following massive destruction. He consulted his Mayan cult friends about Fionn's absence of a recollection of their possible joint exposure to asbestos in Clontarf thirty years ago. His friends were ad idem that men like Fionn, who had lived a fulfilling life steeped in achievements, rarely would recall bad experiences. Alternatively, as a carpenter for many years prior to becoming a woodwork teacher, problems like the one in Clontarf may not have been the rarity it had been for Fergus. They also claimed that if Fionn had in fact been exposed to asbestos, as Fergus now believed, then that event was a negative black swan event foretelling life-altering consequences for both him and his brother Fionn.

He then sought, as he often did in times of personal crisis, the wisdom of the Dalai Lama. "Man sacrifices his health in order to make money. Then he sacrifices money to recuperate his health. Then he is so anxious about the future he does not live in the present or the future; he lives as if he is never going to die, and then dies having never lived."

However, like some thirty million Americans, Fergus had no health insurance and no money to sacrifice on cancer treatment if a medical exam revealed he was a carrier of asbestos particles, a thirty-year-old ticking bomb. In any event, his Internet research suggested asbestos caused cancers when they emerged from smouldering, and they were so virulent they defied all odds of a cure no matter the treatment endured. Unlike Fionn, he had lived his life with unfulfilled dreams, always hoping the best was yet to come. Finally, he consoled himself with the philosophy of the Wild Irish Rover and sang out, "I'll eat when I'm hungry and drink when I'm dry and if that doesn't kill me, I'll live till I die." That night he went to bed full of Bushmills spirits wondering whether he would be a witness in 2012 to the unfolding of the Mayan prophecies; whether his creative inspiration would finally flow before then, and he would get to create an artistic masterpiece; or whether asbestos cancer would take him out before either of such events.

I had agreed to rendezvous with Fionn in Howth, a sleepy fishing village most weekdays which comes alive on weekends to Dubliners escaping from the rat race to enjoy nature at its best on scenic cliff walks. It is also the sleepy village port which enabled the gun smuggling that made the pivotal 1916 Easter Rising for Irish Independents possible. We had spent a lot of boyhood summer time in Howth on its overcrowded beach and traipsing around the village and fishmonger shops. But that day, Fionn had arranged a private yacht excursion for us out to and around Ireland's Eye, a summer paradise for naturists, young lovers, skinny-dippers, and sun worshipers. The closest view I had ever had of this piece of the Auld Sod was from Howth's east pier lighthouse.

I was alone with Fionn for the last time on that yacht excursion. The winds were gusty and the sea was icy cold, which caused mixed emotions from teeth chattering and spinal shivers. His body was by then virtually a shadow skeleton of my younger brother. Yet a great life force sparkled in his dusky eyes. Then his hat was blown off. We looked at each other telepathically.

"I know a man, and his hat blew off!" Fionn beamed in reply.

"What man?"

"A man called Who Do."

"Who Do?"

"I do."

"You do what?"

"I know a man, and his hat blew off!"

We tittered, recalling this party prank of our father once upon a time when we were two little boys. Immediately I saw Fionn clearly in my mind's eye in his short pants standing in the centre of the kitchen singing "Sailor" ("Sailor stop your roaming, Sailor leave the sea, Sailor when the tide turns, Come home safe to me"). And then she was upon us in all her enchantress glory—Ireland's Eye, like an earth mother island with eyes in the back of her head watching everything on the mainland and beyond. It was indeed a eureka moment, but whilst I awaited my epiphany, Fionn broke her enchanting spell by declaring what he would most miss in times to come: not being there to give his daughter away, and not being there to experience his grandchildren. Neither I nor Ireland's Eye could answer his spirit of pining, so we sailed back to the yacht club below an ominous sky but heartened by a panoramic view of Howth's majestic coastline and the feast of salmon and Guinness that awaited us.

Fergus was elated with news that Fionn had survived an arduous lung operation, had undergone extensive chemotherapy, and was hopeful for remission. Fergus was buoyed by their long-distance phone chat, which related the excursion to Ireland's Eye as this provided an entree for them to relive their many happy Howth nights at the Abbey Tavern, especially when the Wolf Tones or the Dubliners had been playing. When he hung up, he recalled a day in Howth he had ventured upon Balscadden House where W. B. Yeats had spent part of his youth and then went on to become the greatest long-lived poet Ireland had produced. For days thereafter, he spent his time surfing on the Internet, and after months of research and soul searching, he came to believe he should adopt the Yeats method of receiving creative inspiration. This would lead him on a spiritual path to find his daimon. The method involved recognising that each man's dreams are antithetical to his lifestyle and that the daimon, or spirit that had been drawn to him or was within him from birth, was one's true and original self. Men like Yeats had become immortalised through gifted works following the recognition and practice of this esoteric philosophy. Fergus discovered the search for the anti-self had also created greats like St Francis of Assisi and Buddha, both of whom had abandoned their worldly possessions and become immortalised by their great deeds on earth. Yeats, however, had been able to balance the needs of his daimon whilst carrying on a mainstream life, which included founding and managing the famous Abbey Theatre in Dublin and becoming one of Ireland's first Free State senators. It dawned on Fergus that because he had no worldly possessions to be a prisoner of, like St Francis or Buddha had, he should simply proceed to live the life of being a full-time artist and await for his daimon to provide the inspiration for his success. This he did, and by the time he arrived in Ireland for Fionn's wake, though wasted, he had the look and aura of a Confucius with a long, shaped beard to match.

During the night of the day 26 August 2005, Fionn passed. I dreamt of him fully rejuvenated, standing tall at the peak of Ireland's Eye invoking and singing "I'll Be There".

And so when his daughter's wedding invitation arrived a few years later, I was apprehensive until her wedding day. And yes, on that day, within the Celtic Circle of Life, I was reunited with him in Tipperary, in a small church which came alive and at a lakeside wedding feast at Coolbawn—in his daughter's happiness, in his wife's serenity, in his son's cocksureness, in his Anam Cara sister, and all within the gentle embrace of his family circle and circle of friends. And who knows in what other mysterious spiritual ways he was, or is, there?

In his succeeding years, Fergus enjoyed a bohemian lifestyle, though punctuated by numerous emergency visits to his local ER due to blackouts from acute episodes of disequilibrium. He was given a diagnosis for bipolar syndrome and was medicated accordingly. He fretted as to whether the bipolar disorder was caused by asbestos fibres in his brain or whether it resulted from his inner search for his daimon. On days he did not pose for aspiring artists, he spent at the beach creating his own art until one day he was entrapped by the law for alleged loitering. His new Christian circle of friends came to his rescue, and through their intercession, he was eventually returned to his freedom again on 4 July 2012. To help him celebrate, he received a facsimile of his niece Deirdre's immortalisation on canvas of a scene from St Anne's Estate with an admonition for him to heed the immortal poetics of Robert Frost ("The woods are lovely dark and deep, but I have promises to keep and miles to go before I sleep, and miles to go before I sleep"). This brought joy to his heart because St Anne's Estate was his woods, just a ten-minute walk from his boyhood family home, and where he had dreamed his youthful daily impossible dreams and at weekends played goalie on its playing fields. It was during this time of his uplifted spirits that some of his Christian friends took him into the wilderness and recorded his testimony to Jesus Christ, which they published on YouTube in memoriam.

Cometh the day! Cometh the moment! Cometh the man! It was 26 August 2012, the seventh anniversary of the passing of Fionn's seven stars. In the witching hours of that night, Fergus, like a tired matador without a red flag, entered his oceanside neighbourhood arena. A black bull came racing towards him. The coroner certified his death as caused by multiple blunt force injuries and surmised he would have died almost immediately after impact. Yet I saw him nights later in the lotus posture with an angelic mischievous grin on his face in the Celtic Twilight Zone.

And Ireland's Eye had no answer for Fergus's abridged life either, save to suggest that ancient Ireland, through its School of Ageless Wisdom, knew it all, and to see the remains of this exile laid to rest in peace with those of his parents and eldest brother, and nearby the grave of Fionn, at another gathering of their remaining clan.

# Andropause Wake

He had nothing to do but reminisce, so he assumed the corpse posture. It was of no attraction to him that yogis preferred the lotus posture when their life force was leaving. Under the sheet, he relaxed his naked, 60-year-old body. A stone from the summit of the Scalp in Ireland, where he had hiked away his youth, rested upon his navel. The stone on the navel trick had been used by novice Celtic monks to ward off sleep whilst they lay in caves mystically seeking to know the unknowable. His subliminal scalp stone treasure on past time travels had worked like magic. Finally, he secured his red and white neckerchief, also a relic from his Boy Scout days, over his eyes.

To play or not to play? That was his big question, at least for the past twenty years! "If we float into life from orgasm, why not float out on one?" he taunted. "Was that not the ultimate promise of Viagra's marketing? Death by orgasm?" A desirable exit indeed, he believed, but a clear breach of his indoctrination by Christian brothers: "Do nothing you would be ashamed to do in front of your mother." His motive search for ecstasy after ecstasy led him to Yul Bryner's Siam and retirement at 55 from the rat race. Thailand, he sensed, was a modern-day approximation to Tir na mBan (Island of Women) in Irish mythology. In his footprints, he left three Californian ex-wives and one love child, named after the longest river in Ireland. For him, the feeling of falling in love trumped being in wedlock. Eros was a recurring answer to his grail question, "What is my purpose?" His swimwear boutique patrons brought this answer home to him daily, as had his wild oats days as a jeweller's apprentice in Dublin's fair city, where every girl he laid eyes upon was his Molly Malone.

With similar feelings in his ascendancy, he resumed sowing wild oats in Bangkok's "Big Bang for your Buck" fleshpots of Potpong, Soi Cowboy, Nana, and Pattaya until his orgiastic existence was interrupted with "dry runs". In his millionaire heyday, before community property laws reduced his means, he had become hooked on mind-expanding and sensual massage offerings of the Escalin Institute at Big Sur in California. There, he had met an octogenarian sage who revealed an orgasm formula as a key rite for his youth and vitality in addition to proper nutrition, exercise, and meditation. The prescription given to him was as follows.

Age × 2 ÷ 10 = number of days to refrain with the caveat that should one empty one's fountain of youth more often, an inexorable premature demise would follow

With that counsel recalled, he retreated to Pee Pee Island. There, he reconnected with Yeats and appreciated differently his poetic Innisfree lines: "There midnights all a glimmer, and noon a purple glow, and evening full of the linnet's wings." At times he wondered whether he had come to understand the ecstatic claims of saintly mystics when they boasted they had been with the angels! It seemed unspoilt nature and exuberant sex every 11.6 days could work miracles on the human psyche.

Fully rejuvenated, he set out for Phuket to consult its resident matchmaker on the dos and don'ts of buying a virgin bride. This was the recommended end game for men of his age sect in Thailand based upon guru claims that young virgin love sustained longevity.

The web of planning and financial negotiation to meet a virgin bride prospect postponed that attraction. Meanwhile, there was fun, food, and fornication attractions in abundance at Phuket's beach resorts to while away his days. Thus, by happenstance or the luck of the Irish, he met the love of his life. Their life together in the Thai countryside is a blur of sexual bliss because his communications were all quixotic. After it ended, he reached out to family and friends on a pilgrimage to his homeland. He talked of becoming a monk in Glennstal Abbey, of working with the Red Cross in Africa, or of joining the travelling people. But all such talk was fleeting imaginations for his restless idle time. And then he was gone again.

Called or not, his power animal appeared at a portal nightly at eleven to service his fancy. For years he had experimented in journeying with drumming or rattles, hares, owls, horses, and sheepdogs. Then he consulted on referral a shaman on methodology for journeying into non-ordinary reality. In those shamanic tutorial sessions, he was introduced to his Irish wolfhound spirit as his new journeying power animal. In the years that followed, he roamed with gusto to the underworld, where he met Fomorians and Fir Bolg, hung out with the merry warriors of Sherwood Forest, chased leprechauns for pots of gold, did Irish jigs with fairies, drank poteen with banshees, feasted at Avalon banquets, and met Brian Boru at the Battle of Clontarf. In the upper world, he flew amongst the stars and floated in the Milky

Way. But most times his spirit animal took him to carouse in the many and varied sex havens around the world, or to unwind in primordial chanting on mountain peaks, or to relax on nude beaches or in the shade at five-star nudist resorts.

During his soul retrieval days on Pee Pee Island, he was inspired to request his wolfhound spirit for a meeting with an Irish goddess. From Pee Pee they departed into the night sky. In a twinkle they were in Killarney, standing in awe of the Paps of Danu. He followed the wolfhound into a dark tunnel at the foot of the Paps, walked towards a distant illuminating light, and emerged into a forest shrouded in green mist.

An echoing voice instructed him, "For your three cauldrons, ask only three questions."

"Whom or what do I serve?" he called out his grail question.

> I am Danu of Nature's Infinity,
> The Tuatha De Dannan know and live,
> The Fountain of Nature is within you,
> As above, So Below,
> Know the Green Tablet, Know Thyself.

"I need answers, not riddles. Whom do I serve?"

"The eternal cycle of life, death, and renewal is not a riddle. To choose Eros over Thanatos is the key, not the quest."

"But I did choose Eros?"

"You were bewitched. But each moment is a curve on the endless knot of time. Retreat, renew, and find your original self."

It was past midnight when the wolfhound barked at him from the portal. That was in vain because he had given a final thanks to his spirit friend for all the journeying and for returning him safely time and time again. Their journey to the Goddess Danu would be their last.

He removed the stone from his navel and the neckerchief from his eyes, took the cup containing his last supper from the bedside table, and swallowed it. No doubt knowing the Celts always took care of their dead, with feelings of nostalgia and gumption, he departed for the Otherworld.

# The Namesake

Declan O'Keefe was a routine, quiet man. There he was at the tail end of his last sabbatical to Victoria Falls, and what had been the point of it all? To rediscover himself? To find his inner man? Or simply to escape the limitations of his ordinary life? Renouka, his barren East Indian wife of forty-three years, had died without fuss one year before to the day. Since then, he had smoked 7,280 cigarettes, drunk 1,092 whiskeys, eaten 1092 square meals, drank 2912 glasses of water and 1082 cups of tea, had 364 nights of sleep, had 365 eliminations, and had 364 daydreams. Now, with his working life done in Zambia, it was time to complete the circle and return to his Dublin cradle to await transportation to heaven. He had returned to the Falls, from where his year had begun, to say goodbye. But it would not beckon to him again as it had on his first sighting forty-five years before.

"Doctor Livingstone I presume?" This, maybe, was because he was now mourning the death of his best friend, Eamon O'Connell.

The day before Eamon O'Connell had committed suicide,

he had given Declan his hill-walking notebook and a sealed envelope to be delivered in person to his brother Sean on his return to Ireland. Some fifty years before his suicide, Eamon had immigrated to England. After three years of roughing it in Liverpool, his luck changed when he was recruited by Roan Consolidated Mines, and he had spent the remainder of his life in Zambia's Copperbelt, never to set eyes on Ireland again. Declan had met the affable Eamon at the Mufulira Golf and Country Club, where they'd wiled away their spare time. He was a lapsed Celtic Catholic turned pagan and was mightily fond of his drink. He tried to balance this weakness as an "early to bed, early to rise" fanatic. At every sunrise, he took an air bath to worship the sun as a son of the sun. At every sundown, he went hill walking. In between these tasks and copper mining, he spent his time at the golf club eating, drinking, and playing. He had never married, but amongst Mufulira's expatriate community, he was well regarded as a renowned polygamist with African beauties, amongst whom he had distributed all his worldly possessions before he kicked the bucket.

On the flight from Lusaka to Heathrow, Declan passed the time studying Eamon's hill-walking notebook. He had committed his suicide on his seventieth birthday, and the notebook had an entry for every day of his sixty-ninth year. The notes, mainly lamentations, were all about his love for Deirbhile, his erstwhile teenage sweetheart. She was a blue-eyed, red-haired goddess whose beauty cast a spell, a spirit of desire, over all who laid eyes upon her. Whilst growing up, Eamon and Deirbhile had monopolised each other's time. But when she transmuted into a beatifical maiden, she desired more and more to be alone, to walk in the shadows. Her aloofness broke his heart and turned his spirit of desire into a spirit of melancholy till he could suffer no more.

Then reluctantly she confided in him that she had "the calling", so he went into exile.

At Heathrow, Declan was suddenly seized by what he now recognised to be Eamon's death wish. On the spur of that moment, he rescheduled the homeward leg of his journey from Dublin to Shannon. From there he hired a car and headed for Belmullet, the hometown of Eamon, forever the Mayo man. By nightfall he reached Ballina, where he decided to overnight because in memory of Eamon, he was moved to not set his eyes on the Belmullet Peninsula until sunrise.

Sure enough, as Eamon regularly boasted, the sun shined there with a special glow, or so it seemed to Declan as he stood at the break of dawn at the Peninsula's stump for an umbilicus joining her to the motherland and paid his respects to Eamon and his sun. At 9 a.m., after a hearty Belmullet Irish breakfast, Declan entered the premises of Sean O'Connell, Victualler, and introduced himself. No sooner had Sean opened and read Eamon's letter than he collapsed to the floor and died in his wife's arms. During that brief eternity, Declan was doubly shocked by the contents of Eamon's letter, which lay sunny side up next to Sean's monstrous feet.

14 August 1976

Sean,

Tomorrow I commit suicide on my seventieth birthday. I know you raped Deirbhile at Fallmore on 15 August 1921.

See you in hell!
Eamon

Before calling for help, Brigid O'Connnell read the letter, stuffed it into her apron, and ordered Declan not to budge. Within minutes, the parish priest, the doctor, and an entourage of neighbours arrived into the shop. Dr Maol's impromptu post-mortem determined Sean's cause of death was his ailing heart, but not before Father Fitzpatrick had administered the last rites. All present then arranged Sean's laying out in the parlour to await his wake and burial arrangements. After that, everybody repaired to the kitchen for tea and sandwiches, where Declan was finally introduced by Brigid to the busybodies as "Eamon's best friend who had brought the sad news of Belmullet's prodigal son's suicide in Zambia, of all places, which had caused poor Sean's final fatal heart attack." When all in the gathering had said their long goodbyes and condolences for the day, Brigid O'Connell ordered Declan to take them to Fallmore Church.

Fallmore lies at the southern tip of the desolate Belmullet Peninsula. When they arrived at the church, Brigid broke their silence to explain that the church and well were dedicated to Saint Deirbhile, who was a sixth-century saint. She noted that the well offers pilgrims a cure for their eye problems, particularly on Saint Deirbhile's feastday, 15 August, adding, "Saint Deirbhile was so beautiful, she had to pluck out her eyes so that no man would desire her and she could dedicate her life to God." Declan was further struck dumb to learn that Eamon's sweetheart, named after Saint Deirbhile, was Brigid's younger sister.

On the drive back to Brigid's, she lamented that her sister Deirbhile was awful lovely; that her infatuation with Saint Deirbhile had lost her to Eamon and the world; that Eamon himself was too immature to accept her calling and had run away demented, never to be seen or heard from again until Declan had arrived with his letter; and that Deirbhile had become a cloistered nun and by now probably had succumbed to senile dementia, as nuns do, but they wouldn't be told anything until she was dead. Having gotten all of that off her chest, Brigid waited until they arrived at her home to say, "As to the rape of my sister, well, in those days there was a spate of hush-hush rapes throughout County Mayo, but no reports were ever made to the Gardaí because that's how we dealt with rape in those days—we didn't. As to Eamon's notion that Sean had raped Deirbhile, well, I doubt it. My poor Sean was impotent throughout his sorry excuse for an adult life, so he took me, a frigid ugly duckling, for his wife. Anyways, our matchmaker thought we were well matched, and sure wouldn't you know it, the fecking crone, the rip was right. Come on in now, Declan. I'll put the kettle on, and we'll have a nice cuppa tea."

# The Headhunt

The five-star world myth and hype that surrounded her said she was the seventh child of a seventh son. Having broken a mystical male power line, Grace O'Malley, aged 12, eloped as a wanderer until she returned aged 50 and founded OranMór retreats. Now ninety, she presided over thirteen OranMór retreats located in remote locations around the world.

The day his father died, Robert "Bobby" Burns started running for his life. It was in his genes! Burns men of his clan lineage all died in their 50s. True to his youthful vows, he had avoided marriage and the desire to reproduce, and at age 40 he ended his working life upon resignation from Amanresorts after fifteen five-star extraordinary years in its soul scape. He told nobody, not even Aman's maestro, about the daimon within which drove his decision, only that he wished to spend the balance of his life in the land of his youth. Six months into navel-gazing at his Wicklow abode, the call came: OranMór retreats needed a COO, and according to Michael Murphy of Goodbodys, Bobby Burns was on the hit list. He agreed to a meeting at the Shelbourne Hotel for "exploratory discussions". His reluctance to do so subsided, urged on by an auto suggestion that a day out in Dublin would do him a world of good.

Michael Murphy had pumped him about the inner workings of Amanresorts and the reason or reasons for his resignation. Frank Prendergast, the outgoing chief operating officer of OranMór, whom Bobby Burns observed as a cherubic fifty-something, was in attendance as an observer only. To be cordial, Bobby Burns had stirred the conversation, so as not to waste their time, into a laudatory exposé of the various Amanresorts in the Aman world stable and the joys they provided the guests to regroup, rethink, recharge. He graciously declined Frank Prendergast's invitation to lunch at Bewleys in favour of a spiritual stroll in St Stephens Green. But more so, it was to confirm his retirement as an irrevocable personal act. He was astonished three days later when Grace O'Malley's letter arrived, inviting him to meet her at OranMór I on Clare Island.

Clare Island in Clew Bay, from a history of Ireland, had been part of the territories of the O'Malley clan, made famous by their daughter Grace O'Malley with her notoriety as a pirate queen. How could he refuse? He dashed off his reply, confirming he would be at the Roonah Quay at 8 a.m. on 8 August for pick-up by the OranMór ferry. He added he wished to be back to the mainland by 6 p.m. because he had reserved a room at the Clew Bay Hotel for 7–8 August. This reservation was made after he had fantasised about Grace O'Malley the enigmatist of OranMór retreats, and the legend that Clew Bay was still ruled by Grace O'Malley, the notorious sixteenth-century pirate queen. He was under no illusion that his fantasy had been sparked by his risk aversion instincts to happenstance. Nevertheless, he opted to return to mainland terra firma rather than spend the night out to sea on Clare Island. In any case, common sense dictated that if he stayed over, he coveted the COO position.

When he checked into the Clew Bay Hotel, the receptionist greeted him with the statement, "You are the man off to OranMór in the morning." When he asked her how she knew that, she said, "The ferry master spent time at the hotel today whilst he waited for Grace to return from Knock." From their exchange, he learnt anytime Grace O'Malley was in residence at OranMór, she made a day pilgrimage to Knock, where the Virgin Mary, St Joseph, and St John had appeared in 1879. According to the receptionist, "Grace is known in these parts to be very partial to St John, but no one seems to know what sort of miraculous healing she's seeking when she visits the Knock Shrine."

Bobby Burns found the ferry master full of platitudes but no useful information during the fifteen-minute voyage to Clare Island. There, he was planted with his day bag and the assurance the ferry master would return for him at 5.05 p.m. "After your afternoon tea to take you back." He then followed an OranMór I valet to the O'Malley cottage.

On the whitewashed wall of the thatched cottage, a plaque read, "Terra Mariq Potens O'Malley—O'Malley, powerful on land and sea."

"It was given to me by a powerful political Taoiseach pal after I obtained planning permission for OranMór. It is a replica of a memorial on the O'Malley tomb here on Clare Island, where my reputed ancestors and namesake are interred," said Grace O'Malley as she welcomed him. At once he was captivated by her carriage, her luminous presence, and her warmth when they shook hands. After agreeing to call each other Grace and Bobby, he followed her to her inner sanctum. There, in its sparseness, he was confronted by a fierce portrait of a timeless George Bernard Shaw hung over a plaque with his immortal warning: "Youth is wasted on the young."

Their morning together evaporated with reminiscences of Grace's visits to Amanresorts and her admission that her first visit to Amandari in Bali was an inspiration to create OranMór retreats. At length, she explained how, since Frank Prendergast had become an octogenarian, he wished to retire from his world travel schedule to manage OranMor XIII.

Consequently, Goodbodys had been engaged to help find a successor. When Bobby, in disbelief, queried Frank Prendergast's age, Grace laughingly explained that Frank was a devotee of Moses who actually lived 136 years despite the three score and ten life span reference in the Bible, which she claimed was a lament for humankind's premature demise and not a death sentence. Grace then provided an overview of OranMór retreats' equity model. Currently, there were thirteen OranMór retreats and thirteen equal OranMór partners. A prerequisite to become a partner was to fund an OranMór retreat. The admission price into the partnership was indeed substantial, but the dividends of partners was priceless. Presently, to complete the OranMór world stable of retreats, there was room for only two more partners because OranMór did not intend to grow beyond fifteen retreats. Therefore, Grace planned within the next five years two new OranMór retreats to be added by two new incoming partners.

For lunch, haggis was served, with Grace explaining it had been specially flown in from the Shetland Islands to whet Bobby Burns's appetite. She added that since she'd discovered it, she found the poetry of Robert Burns full of the music of life. She believed that was what Scotsmen actually celebrated annually at Burns Supper. She teased Bobby Burns to discover the poetics of his namesake Robert Burns. Then she left him to his daydreams and to ramble around OranMór I at his leisure, and he had the key to Inishglora Cottage to relax until 4 p.m., when they would meet again at the O'Malley cottage for afternoon tea.

His wellness regime included taking a brisk walk after lunch and then a nap, lying down on his left side for about twenty minutes. "Good for your heart," according to his doctor. And so he set out on Grace's suggested ramble. His mind raced. Grace could not be 90! Frank could not be 80! Was there a hidden secret within OranMór, within its upmarket wellness and rejuvenation hyperbole? Slowly his sojourn in OranMór's nature gardens brought him to his senses. "Relax and soak up its energy for what it is, not for any inherent meanings," he told himself. He was enthralled as he walked in circles about the thatched cottages laid out in three clusters of five. The simplicity of it all with winds gusting in all directions and the marvels of the heavens above brought him a tranquillity he had not experienced before. When he found and entered the Inishglora cottage, his mind was at ease. Its entrance greeting read, "The island of Inishglora is where the children of Lir spent their last three hundred years of exile as swans. It is said their voices melted the hearts of all who heard them sing." He lay down on the bed on his left side and waited for his heart to melt.

In his 1881 *Portrait of a Lady*, Henry James revealed, "Under certain circumstances there are few hours in life more agreeable than the hour dedicated to the ceremony known as afternoon tea." Since Grace O'Malley had discovered that as a truism in Hong Kong, she had practiced the rite of taking afternoon tea. That day it was a fitting end to her due diligence of Bobby Burns. They both glowed with life as time seemed to stand still, and all could be said or not said through smiles and the sounds of OranMór blowing in the wind.

Ultimately, Bobby Burns was at ease to ask the question that had burned in his heart since he had met her. "Grace, what is the secret of your exquisite longevity?" He memorised her answer for deep consideration.

"OranMór, as you know, is our Celtic heritage mantra for the music of life. My ancestors all lived in the spirit of the Holy Grail! That spirit is my birthright. I enjoy passing the spirit of long life to my initiated OranMór partners. We pray our guests find that spirit at our OranMór retreats."

When the offer arrived from Goodbodys, he unreservedly accepted the job. Grace had told him her counterpart at Amanresorts had highly recommended him for the position with a rider that "All Bobby Burns is searching for is a new lease on life." That was true! His had been a restless retirement. Not even his regular hiking days in the Wicklow Mountains could quiet his restlessness. Perhaps he had acted prematurely. Ten years now seemed a long time to await a genetic terminal attack whilst trying to make a life. His acceptance was also tinged with hope that nine years with OranMór could add years to his life. His transition to that new life was scheduled to take place at OranMór XIII in the Belham Valley of Montserrat, the Emerald Isle of the Caribbean.

He had landed at Blackheath Airport. From there he was whisked to OranMór XIII and spent the night well protected in its Sheela Na Gigs cabin. At 3 a.m., he arose jet-lagged to view from its veranda the thirteen partners of OranMór emerge, who had gathered for their annual retreat and to whom he was to be introduced during breakfast at the Great House. Each one sat in the lotus posture and together formed a circle from aurora until sunrise. Then he watched them disperse to their cabins, each one an ageless, agile, mysterious woman. He needed no more self-convincing. He was now certain OranMór owners shared a perpetual youth philosophy. Perhaps even the secret to the Fountain of Youth had been discovered by Grace in her days as a wanderer. A secret he hoped would be revealed to him soon. That, he intuitively knew, was the reason he had accepted the job.

Then the Soufriere Hills volcano erupted!

The OranMór evacuation plan was implemented flawlessly, culminating in their OranMór ferry delivering them safely to Antigua. There, Frank Prendergast would remain to deal with the aftermath of the natural disaster in his new role as resident manager of OranMór XIII, with the certain conviction the designers had gotten it right and his chosen retreat would suffer no harm. Grace's twelve majestic partners boarded flights to return to their private lives. Grace departed for Nepal to turn the first sod for OranMór XIV in the Himalayas. Bobby Burns flew off to the Isle of Man, the commercial centre of OranMór retreats, to take up his new position as its COO, energised with excitement and adventure for an extraordinary long life to come even if, in the poetics of his namesake, he was left only with "peace and pain for promised joy."

# Mother's Wake

When her death call came, I was a student of recurrent nightmares: that my mother was not my real mother. The most haunting remembered detail was of my godmother leading me as a boy, by the ears, on a long walk through a pitch-dark tunnel into a candlelit sitting room to face a woman dressed in black from head to toe and seated in an armchair. None of her facial features were made present to me because she wore a laced black hat and a veil. Then my godmother, a spinster sister of my mother who helped rear me, announced, "This is your real mother." The preludes to my nightmares may have varied, but the final confrontation scene remembered was always the same following startled resurrections.

The pilgrimage home to wake my mother was a long one from Dominica to Boston to London to Dublin. Too much time to be alone. Too much time to think.

In my travels, I regressed from melancholy to a kitchen scene at age 12. We were smoking cigarettes and drinking tea whilst choosing horses to bet on. I was studying form, but my mother was studying names because she always chose her bets by the names she fancied. That day she fancied Kathleen Rua. Given her long-established affinity and attraction to winning names, be they jockeys' or horses' names, I asked her how she had come to call me Kieron. Whilst she reflected on that trick question, I teased her over her apparent lapse in naming protocol amongst her eight children, reminding her that my four brothers and three sisters all had middle names but I had none. I was just Kieron, a middle child without a middle name! Amused, she related to me how the bus had broken down and lost its bonnet on the way to my baptism, and how we had arrived at Marino Church all hot and bothered and very late. The priest was agitated too but proceeded to baptise me Kieron anyway, that being my mother's chosen Christian name for me. She was adamant I had no middle name because she was sure Kieron was good enough for me. To press home her point, she chided me that Kieron meant a sod of turf, and sure wasn't I spending all my waking hours running back and forth to turf accountants' shops or at horse racing courses. Then, perhaps to sow more ambitious seeds, she informed me that the priest who'd baptised me had prophesied, "Your Kieron will travel the world." She died suddenly twenty-two years later in my thirty-fourth degree of death. But that day, like so many of my childhood days, was filled with joy. Even Kathleen Rua, whom we both backed, romped home a winner.

Before I awoke in Boston, I saw in a rainforest mist a beautiful face adorning hypnotic blue eyes. She wore an emerald green hooded cape. She was beckoning to me to come to her and whispering "K-E-R-I-O-N" as a mantra through her scarlet red lips. As I moved closer to her, I woke up.

There had been no time to dwell on my Bostonian goddess dream until I was seated for take-off to London. By then I had drifted back into a state of melancholy or a spirit of longing to be home. Meandering thoughts led me to Brother Devine, one of numerous Christian brothers who had indoctrinated me in boyhood. He was the first to enlighten me I was named after Saint Ciaran, the Irish spelling for the Anglo Kieron. Saint Ciaran, he had related, was a great scholar in Christendom who had established great seats of learning. Brother Devine assured me I could do no better than to try to follow in Saint Ciaran's footsteps. However, when I learnt the patron saint of Ireland, Saint Patrick, had outdone Saint Ciaran by banishing all the snakes from Ireland, and had cracked the trinity code with the shamrock, I moved on to alternative boyhood heroes discovered in poetry lessons: Milton, Yates, Shelley, Burns, and Wordsworth.

The thump on touchdown at Heathrow rescued me from a spine-chilling nightmare: my Bostonian muse transformed into a hag, a crone, or a Sheela-na-gig. I was not sure which because she was draining the living daylights out of me when the plane landed. I held my Celtic cross and gave thanks to God that I was back on terra firma. Then my godmother posed me a question from her grave. "Are you sorry now you replaced your lovely Saint Christopher medal for a pagan Celtic cross around your neck? Sure wouldn't you have had safer passage across the Atlantic with the patron saint of travellers?"

Then I heard my father speak: "Are you glad you're not sorry, Kieron?" With the fear my mind fast becoming a madhouse, I deplaned.

Fortunately, on those questions there was no time to dwell because I dashed to the Aer Lingus gate to take a connecting flight to Dublin. From Dublin Airport, I was whisked to the undertaker's, arriving just in time to join family and friends for the closing of the coffin. Gathered around the oak coffin were only yellow faces dressed in black, full of sobbing and wailing and casting of eyes for the last time on my mother. She had been a listening, caring, and loving mother to all her children and all who had crossed her path. If my godmother was right, those who touched or kissed their departed loved one's remains would enjoy only everlasting good memories of them. In that superstitious knowledge, I kissed my mother goodbye for the last time. A heartbreaking moment became an epiphany, dawning upon me there and then. I had not had the opportunity, when my godmother died of a brain tumour, to practice what she had preached on her. "Sure isn't that why I'm haunting you day and night, you fecking eejit," retorted my godmother.

My first supper back in holy Ireland, the island of saints and scholars, followed a church service to receive my mother's remains from the undertaker. That family gathering relived my mother's end times and our grandest childhood memories of her. The family doctor had maintained her in fine fettle as her caregiver. Like him, she had quit white sugar because he believed it was the deadliest of all daily Dublin drugs. Be that as it may, for all her years after quitting the white lady, she enjoyed heartful health despite being slowly worn down with painful arthritis and the ageing process. When the witching hour descended upon us, I reluctantly prepared to depart to the vanishing family home. It was at that juncture of the night that my sister related how she had gone through Mammy's keepsakes and found "Of all things, Kieron's Rotunda birth tag." It recorded my birth in cold statistics: the ward number, the date, the time, the weight in pounds and ounces, the sex, and the name: Kerion. My facial expression of fascination must have turned shocking. My shock quickly evaporated with a sisterly hug and a parting suggestion: "You might frame that for posterity."

For a while, as I lay in bed, I thought of my father alone in the master bedroom. Then I regressed to a debate with my mother after I had obtained my birth certificate to apply for a passport to embark upon a working sabbatical in Zambia. The issue was whether I should traipse all the way back to the Custom House to have the misspelling of my name corrected or rely upon my mother's advice: "Sure galloping horses won't see it." I went ahead with my passport application, and sure enough, they spelt Kieron in the passport as it was spelt in the passport application, not Kerion as it appeared on the accompanying birth certificate submitted in evidence of my bona fides. Alone time and lingering inquisitiveness in Africa caused me to do some research. It turned out Kerion was a serpentine name denoting one of the serpent sea people of the Atlantean fire god. His Eirin issue, the Druids, were reputed to be the serpents whom St Patrick exoterically banished from pagan Ireland as snakes. I recalled resolving how on my return home, I would go straight to the Custom House and get a proper birth certificate. God knows why I never did! Had I, I would have discovered much sooner there was no misspelling of my name on my birth certificate; the ward tag found in my mother's keepsakes was proof positive of that. I wanted to unravel this riddle that night, but inner turmoil and outer howling gales conked me out till daybreak.

Mother's send-off to heaven was a Latin Mass in St Bridgid's Church, Killester. Her coffin stood before the altar as an offering for a life well lived. The church full with family, friends, neighbours, and daily Mass-goers. I was given the honour to read the epistle, but I broke with commoner protocol and also read a eulogy. In doing so, I was of course guilty of the first deadly sin, pride in my mother. Standing there before the coffin, I felt the winter chills of the cold church and had to grind my teeth hard to control the spirit of loss within my cells. When I finished my script and the epistle, I looked out upon the multitude and was sure I saw my Boston green lady in the church doorway blessing herself from the holy water font, but the priest nudged me to return to my pew before I was certain. Kneeling there, I was overcome with uncontrollable chattering and shivering. The cemetery was also bitterly freezing cold. Indeed, had the tears shed around the descent of the coffin not been wiped away by white handkerchiefs, they may have turned to icicles upon all the grieving faces. Redemption came only when the dust was settled and the wreaths were laid. Then the chosen many escaped to a fire-warmed family home for the remains of the day, comforted with lashings of sandwiches, cakes, and pots of tea.

Without sympathisers, I embarked upon a midnight stroll through St Anne's estate. It was illuminated by a full moon as I walked alone from the Killester end to the Clontarf end. Then I sat in awesome wonder amongst a grove of trees, my favourite area of St Anne's woods since boyhood. "I am Dana Divine, Mother of the Tuatha de Dannan," my Boston goddess said, replacing the great tree that had been before me. I was stupefied. I knew that she knew I knew all about the mythology of the Tuatha de Dannan, the people of serpent wisdom, the prediluvian inhabitants of Ireland who had retreated underground, shape-shifting to fairies to escape massacre by marauding invaders. All she transmitted to me that night was that she was my divine mother too. I was conceived under the sign of Aquarius and born under the sign of the Phoenix, renamed Scorpio since ancient times, with a golden brown birthmark and the serpent name Kerion, tweaked for me by her to open the way for me to be born again to help pave the way with other like-minded druidic outsiders for the return from the Otherworld of the life, the light, and the way of the Tuatha de Dannan culture in the Age of Aquarius. She descended away, asseverating, "The twenty-first century will be matriarchal, or it will not be."

# The Well

I watched them leave from the hall door, my six boys and Kevin, my stud of a husband, off on another weekend camp. *Good riddance,* I thought as I slammed the door.

It seemed like an eternity since I'd walked down the aisle, but it wasn't. Back then, I was a 21-year-old virgin goddess, and now I was a 33-year-old frigid vessel. I had tried to escape before, back to my budding stage career. But Kevin had tracked me down in London and brought me back only to "piss me knickers" during a family rosary reunion. I had learnt my lesson: my next escape must be permanent. Preparation required a day asleep and a night awake. After a feast of rashers, eggs, sausages, black-and-white pudding, and fried brown soda bread, all washed down with two cups of tea, I crawled into bed.

I wondered again how me mother coped with it all for so long—the endless cooking, washing, ironing, cleaning, and skivvying. There had been eight of us growing up, seven brothers and me, plus me daddy. I should have asked her! But when me daddy died suddenly, me mother departed one night into the Liffey only to be fished out the next day, dead as a doornail.

That was my last semiconscious thought when the alarm went off at 5.30 p.m. I got up, did me ablutions, and went downstairs for tea and toast. At 6 p.m., on my way back upstairs, I took my prayer from behind the Sacred Heart, sat in Kevin's rocker, and read it again like the first time.

> Some nights stay up till dawn as the moon sometimes does for the sun,
> Be a full bucket pulled up the dark way of a well then lifted out into the light.
> Something opens our wings, something makes boredom and hurt disappear. Someone fills the cup in front of us; we taste only sacredness.

It was a prayer from thirteenth-century Persia which had fascinated me since coming across it in the library. Tonight was my opportunity to put it into practice. I sat mindful and rocked. Betwixt and between my dozing and waking hours, there was nothing miraculous to witness. The sounds from outside which infiltrated the house seemed like the usual background noise of daily living, to which I had no time to pay attention. During one snooze, I think I saw the Sacred Heart, but then, that was something I saw several times a day on the landing. Cutting a long night short when the alarm rang at 6 a.m., I felt only the call of me bladder as usual. After tea, half a grapefruit, and cornflakes, I dolled meself up and took the train into Dublin.

It would have been me mother's sixty-fifth birthday had she been living, so I went first to the pro-cathedral and lit a candle. Then I said another decade of the rosary for the repose of her soul. After that, there was nothing to do but mope about till it was time for me elevenses, a chocolate éclair and a nice cuppa. As I looked around whilst holding my tray for an empty table, I couldn't believe me eyes. *Isn't that me Aunty Jude sitting all alone at the corner table, whom I haven't seen in donkey's years? It is, to be sure!*

"Aunty Jude, fancy meeting you here!"

"Well, aren't you a sight for sore eyes? The spittin' image of your mother, God rest her soul!"

We chatted galore until it came out that Aunty Jude had spent that day with me mother the day she did herself in. Then there were tears galore! It turned out every year since, Aunty Jude had reenacted that fateful day with me mother, trying to pinpoint what it was she had missed. By coincidence or fate, we had met up at the Kylemore Bakery for tea and chocolate éclairs as they had. Now, Aunty Jude insisted I must celebrate with her me mother's last happy birthday. How could I refuse? We killed an hour, arms linked, strolling in Henry Street until 1 p.m., and then it was up to Woolworth's Cafe for shepherd's pie and apple tart.

For the afternoon, we roamed around Stephen's Green talking, watching, and feeding the ducks. I learnt Aunty Jude had had a few flings in her time but had never met a man with whom she would have wanted to spend the rest of her life. When her menopause arrived, she saw the light with acceptance that one's happiness must come from within. At first she had been angry at having wasted her youth seeking her happiness in the opposite sex, things, and people, when all the time her mother superior at school had been right: "If you can't love yourself, don't expect other people to love you." Though she had made her first Communion at 7 on reaching the age of reason, she was pissed off as a victim of religion and hormones, which had kept her from using that reason before menopause. Since then, she had been able to put all life's hurts, false promises, loves, and hates behind her, and she became a spiritual adventurer. Now retired from a work life in nursing, she lived every day as if it were Sunday. She was staying at the Four Courts Hotel and would be driving home to Kileshandra come the morning. She asked that I stay the night with her rather than return to my empty house. But after dinner in her room, I told her, "I must be about my father's business." We said our goodbyes, and I left her to steep in her own happiness with the assurance I would visit her when I could.

From an old photo of me mother and her mother on a day outing in Dublin, I reckoned me mother may have gone in off the Halfpenny Bridge. She looked like such a happy girl on the bridge in that photo. I scouted the area for the next few hours. In between the scouting, I visited some of Dublin's finest public houses and must have had at least four vodkas and orange to cool me courage. It was coming up to closing time, and a dapper approached and whispered in me ear, "Do you fuck?"

I replied, "You must get smacked on your face a lot!"

Smirking, he said, "Begorra, I do—but I get a lotta fucks too."

I got up, turned me back on the gobshite, and walked out into the night.

On the Halfpenny Bridge, I came to the conclusion I would have reached sooner had I not spent the day with Aunty Jude: it was not practical to go in off the bridge for the next few hours because someone would see me climbing the rails and might call 999. Instead, I decided I should sit on the embankment wall and await a quiet moment to freefall backwards into the Liffey. Then I saw Aunty Jude trotting towards me, arms reaching out till we embraced. She said, "Your mother will never be dead whilst you are alive." I burst into uncontrollable weeping. She led me off the embankment over to the Four Courts Hotel and up to her room.

We lay on the bed in a life-lock cuddle, silent till morning. Prompted or not by the Holy Ghost, I asked, "How did you know?"

"I knew," said she, "because I sensed the rut within you, the same creature of boredom that drove your poor mother to her wits' end." She had hoped she was wrong, but to be on the safe side, she had followed me from her hotel. As the night wore on, she awaited divine inspiration to intervene. She begged me to return home with her until I would recover my spirit élan. She promised to teach me her art of living, her secret life as a creature of her mind. I agreed.

On the way to Kileshandra, we had to stop at my home to tidy up and leave a note for Kevin to tell him where I was. Upon returning my prayer to the Sacred Heart, I trembled in thinking it had been answered, and Aunty Jude had become my guardian angel.

# Rose Vale

Until the first dawn I went to ring the St Bridgid's Church angelus bell, I had never crossed her at dawn. At dusk, having rung the angelus bell, she was a haunting shortcut home. As an 11-year-old neophyte altar boy with the fear of God in me, I could sense the banshees in the pitch darkness of Rose Vale. Her narrow pathway was some five hundred paces, with a ditch flowing below her dipping midway. Grotesque trees, nettles, and other weeds adorned her banks, and ice-cold gusting winds flew through her right, left, and centre. One never could see her hounds, but their erotomania howling was frightening.

That first dawn and every angelus dawning thereafter on my roster, until he was taken away, we crossed paths at about 5.55 a.m. My first dark sighting of his satanic, imposing structure scared me silly until he became human. My mother told me, "That would be Mr Stewart, who lives two doors up." Mrs Stewart had told her he did night security work.

My scout troop chaplain said Mr Stewart was an agnostic.

My research said an agnostic was "one of those persons who disclaim any knowledge of God or of the origin of the universe or of anything but material phenomena, holding that with regard to such matters nothing can be known." As an indoctrinated Roman Catholic from birth, I was dumbfounded that such men existed, so I researched Gnostic: "one of a sect that arose in the first ages of Christianity who pretended to be the only men who had a true knowledge of the Christian religion and professed a system of doctrines based partly on Christianity, partly on Greek and Oriental philosophy relating to knowledge, especially esoteric mystical and occult knowledge; Christian heretics of the first to third centuries claiming Gnosis—knowledge of spiritual mysteries." That made me double dumbfounded but fascinated.

The Stewarts were a middle-aged, childless couple who kept to themselves. She was a shoulder-length redhead who dressed plainly without a screed of make-up. They were not in the good books of their neighbours. One neighbour was disgusted to have atheists living next door to her in holy Ireland, as she boasted of having reared her firstborn to become a priest. Another neighbour despised them because they got away to the continent for four weeks every year, and she never went anywhere. The postmistress thought Mr Stewart was a great magnetiser and could not understand how he had ended up with a barren wife whilst she herself had been left on the shelf. Another neighbour fumed at Mr Stewart's comings and goings at all hours of the night, which caused the neighbourhood dogs to bark and denied her a good night's sleep. Anytime another neighbour had a bilious attack, she complained that Mrs Stewart would not share her dietary secrets of keeping weight off, but she noted she was always buying livers and salmon. She was also mortified by Mr Stewart's glowing good health, whereas she had an ailing husband. The newsagent boasted that with six daughters to do the housekeeping and chores, she could put her feet up from morning till night and couldn't understand Mrs Stewart's need to be always traipsing outdoors.

Every Thursday night, when I took the 42A bus to Tara Street baths, Mr Stewart was on it too. Sometimes when it was too cold to go swimming, I followed him. I lost him once in the crowd in the GPO. Another dead end was when I saw him enter the Corinthian Cinema. Most times he just went into cafes or got on another bus. Always at weekends, he was, like me, in the woods walking alone. As my Sherlock Holmes games acting had produced no clues to his agnosticism, I decided to visit his home for bob-a-job week even though my home district had not been allocated to me.

It was after midday when I rang their doorbell. Mrs Stewart opened the door. She was dressed in a pentacle-crested yellow sari with tempts of nothing underneath. There was a lingering smell of incense surrounding her. I could see Mr Stewart down the hallway; he was dressed in yellow pyjamas. Beethoven was playing in the background, I guessed. She told me I could enter through her back gate and mow her lawn. When I was all but finished raking up the grass, Mr Stewart came out and handed me a glass of lemonade. I asked him straight out, "What is it like to be an agnostic?" He queried me as to who had told me he was. I confessed to it being the scout chaplain.

When the raking was finished and it was time for Mr or Mrs Stewart to sign my bob-a-job card, he invited me inside so that he might answer my question. Seated at their kitchen table, Mr Stewart explained that the scout chaplain had gotten it wrong because he was in fact a Gnostic, not an agnostic. When I invited him to tell me more, I learnt that the practice of Gnosticism was a process of self-realisation by obtaining absolute knowledge through personal experience, and that through a self-realisation process one came to know what would remain unknowable to agnostics, priests like the chaplain, and others. He expanded his discourse to proclaim that in order to be self-realised, one must annihilate one's temptations to the seven deadly sins of pride, covetousness, lust, anger, gluttony, envy, and sloth. He told me no more than that, claiming I was too young to commence my search for the Holy Grail. One should be at least 21 to do so. In any event, as a Boy Scout, an altar boy, and a schoolboy, I had enough to occupy myself with.

I asked him if the medallion he wore around his neck was related to his beliefs. Intrigued, he responded, "It is the Viking sign which represents the life force for the path one must follow, not from ulterior motives but from the core of one's individuality." Perhaps sensing my heightened interest, he assured me he would still be around when I reached twenty-one, and if at that time I wished to pursue the Gnostic philosophy further, he would become my mentor.

Months later in the late afternoon, I had crossed Rose Vale without event on my way home from a walk in the woods. I was almost there when the block was suddenly cordoned off by Black Marias. Minutes more, Mr and Mrs Stewart were led out of their home in handcuffs, never to be seen or heard from again. The next day's papers reported he had been a World War II German spy. I wondered then whether his medallion was not in fact some kind of swastika and what other Nazi paraphernalia was found in his home. I wondered too what the postmistress thought of their yellow attire seen below their overcoats because I was sure all the neighbours had witnessed the spectacle of their arrest from behind their window curtains. I was left to wonder because the Stewarts were never spoken about again, at least not by their neighbours in the presence of children.

Having wrestled with these matters for some time, I made

up my mind to refer the data to Skipper for his insights at an opportune time at the next troop meeting. The Stag, Tiger, and Lion patrols had fallen in, but the Skipper was late in calling us to attention for inspection. He was deep in conversation with his quartermaster, the chaplain, and a visiting skipper from a neighbouring troop. Finally, they broke apart, and the Skipper called us to attention. It was the first time I saw grown men with tears in their eyes. With lumps in his throat, Skipper announced President John Fitzgerald Kennedy had been assassinated in Dallas, Texas. He then reminded us of President Kennedy's historic visit to Ireland and how every fellow Irishman had expected him to change the world. The Skipper then called on the chaplain to lead us in prayers for the repose of President Kennedy's soul. After five decades of the rosary, the Skipper dismissed the troop, telling us all to go to our homes because he was feeling too sad to continue the meeting.

Apart from a group of five older scouts who formed a testosterone patrol to roam the village for sightings of girls with whom they were infatuated, most of the troop drifted aimlessly into the night, going in all directions from our scout den.

As I walked into Rose Vale, she was unusually calm, as if her banshees had departed to do their death wailing elsewhere. Unwilling to go home, I sat down in wonderment for three hours. Sometimes I tried to self-realise, and sometimes I debunked the Irish myth that America was the land of opportunity, but mostly my mind was just a blank. From time to time, I was distracted by drunks, lovers, and dog walkers drifting up and down Rose Vale's pathway.

When it was time to give up and go home, the winds picked up. I heard whistling haunts throughout the Vale and chanting something like "So will you" over and over again. Sensing the demonic was afoot, I ran from Rose Vale all the way home.

I learnt from Skipper at the next troop meeting that Gnostic Christians were no better or worse than we Celtic Christians, who also honour our pagan heritage and continue with the practice of our pagan rituals; that scouting was the best training passage to self-realisation in manhood; and that Sowelu (pronounced só-wá-lóó) was the name for the Viking life force insignia on Mr Stewart's medallion.

That night, Skipper and I parted at Rose Vale with the scout's handshake and his riddle.

> In yer search for the Holy Grail, beware, for there are gombeen-gurus, tricksters, and shysters at large on this green earth. Not even our chaplain nor this scout master have found the Philosopher's Stone, until when we are born again. Revieresco—we grow green again.

# Walking on Air

To cut a long, sixty-year story short—was in it, you know, not really An Gorta Mór (the Great Famine) that exiled your man himself to America? No, not really! 'Twas really its aftershocks and risings revolutionising Ireland into a north and south, overpopulated, divided Republic that did that. When all's said and done and truth be told, 'twas a mixture of all them things since 1845 that spawned Ireland's economic, enormous, exiled population. So anyway, to get to the point (the pint's for when I'm finished!), any way you look at it, Lester Byrne counts as one of An Diaspora Mór (the Great Diaspora) out of Ireland.

However, not being interred on Google or one of Irish America's blinkered insiders, Lester is deemed to be a cog like the vast majority of its multinationals daily driving its wheels around and around in its materialistic, merry-go-round, commercial world. Ostensibly in Lester's hobby world, there are, to wit, only winners, losers, and also-rans. Alas, Lester Byrne, after memorable vanished time on earth, now has to cope with diminishing time—the grey times of being 60 and beyond. *To hell with all that, he thought. Nothing another Marlboro and Carlsberg, or a trip back to the back of beyond, the Auld Sod, can't fix.* Besides, Santa Anita was on for his birthday. To be sure, he fancied this omen, part and parcel of his brilliant Irish luck. And so with tools down and family told, he was a rebel again and off to the races.

The sport of kings maintained his youthful inner man and his mindset as a time machine for form, parlance, and legends. A zone of paddocks, grandstands, totes, bookies, majestic horses, leprechaun jockeys, and winners was his nirvana. 'Twas this persona of Lester's which surely created his first sexagenarian epiphany absent the paranormal. And swear to God that's the bleeding truth, you know, behind this tale, absent the blarney. Right?

A demigod, a filly named Vulture whose racing form read "Never flattered" in any of her starts, manifested when she locked her dark eyes on Lester's from across the parade ring. Just like Nijinsky's had, as a god, in 1969. For the umpteenth time, with eyes wide open, Lester watched Nijinsky from Tattenham Corner gallop from sixth in the 1970 Epsom Derby and canter into history, slamming the field. He immediately emptied his clip and went all in on Vulture. She too slammed the also-rans.

They say if you're going through hell, keep on going because you're bound to come out the other side. Be that as it may, Lester Byrne, a vulpine knight gambler, was always walking on air whenever he won, sort of like experiencing a runner's high in the zone. Winning fuelled his spirit. He sensed that spirit much more than ever before when Vulture crossed the winning line.

In common with a groundswell of Irish American patriots, Lester nourished the notion of retiring to Ireland. His dream to do so was kept alive by depositing 50 per cent of all his winnings to his IRA—to wit, his individual retirement account and not the notorious Irish Republican Army spawned by the political partition of Ireland. The Irish exodus had also spawned some thirty-five million inhabitants in America who claimed Irish heritage, who spawned Ireland's heraldic and ancestry tourism industry.

Homeward bound from Santa Anita in his green preowned Jaguar, Lester wondered how many of his generation might get to retire to Ireland and "know the place for the first time", to paraphrase T. S. Eliot. For sure, Lester believed, people needed to believe "the best is yet to come", to paraphrase President Ronald Regan. For "if dreams die first and then the man", to paraphrase Arthur Hailey, Lester was certain his growing IRA nest egg would keep his dreams alive until the end of time.

Back in his private lounge bar, The Weigh Inn, and surrounded by his beloved family, with uisce beatha (holy Irish water), the spirit of the ages, Lester relived his lifetime double epiphany— the Nijinsky one at age twelve, the Vulture one at sixty. It was altogether more than great craic because he now knew, to be sure, he had another sure thing to bet on before his turf time. "Ah, you will," said he. Under the ancient rule of three, the Trinity rule of Gods, the Shamrock rule of Celtic Irish, another brilliant "Go to God" epiphany was yet to come—the trifecta.

# Celibate Affairs

Every night she came to him in the sacristy. He disrobed, manhood erect, she sky-clad and advancing in a cloud of benediction incense smoke, an enigma, flooding his gate of life and death. At 3 a.m. he would awaken from that nightmare engulfed in perspiration, soiled in semen shame. In his mist-walking hours, he called her Dicey Riley in mockery of his mother's favourite melody.

Dr Hyde felt like a new man since his confession the night before. Breakfasting famished, he enticed his wife to make preparations for three weeks in June, their twenty-first anniversary, so they could fly away to Rome for some overdue quality time together. With his proposition reluctantly agreed upon, he walked up the corridor to his surgery at the front of their home to prepare for the morning's patients.

In order of appearances, Dr Hyde doctored to rheumatism, a carbuncle, a pregnancy, an earache, piles, influenza, an STD, and bronchitis. Then in walked Father Devine.

"Father Devine, what a surprise!"

"Dr Hyde, I have come to you with a most delicate matter, as I know now your professional confidentiality will be beyond reproach."

Dr Hyde, blushing, emitted, "Of course! What seems to be the matter?"

A red-faced Father Devine iterated with acute embarrassment how he was suffering from episodes of wet dreams.

To put him at his ease, Dr Hyde related how occasional seminal emissions (once a week) without discomfort or other symptoms is a physiological phenomenon in a male adult unmarried or living apart from his spouse. Therefore, for a celibate priest, weekly nocturnal seminal emissions would be a functional process. However, Dr Hyde realised Father Devine was not comforted, and after having assessed his general demeanour more critically, he added, "Frequent seminal emissions can be a morbid condition often accompanied by dizziness, listlessness, lassitude, emaciation, a loss of memory, aching of the loins, weakness of the legs, and impairment of sleep." Father Devine admitted he was suffering all these side effects more or less. Dr Hyde concluded he would have to perform a general examination. "Frequent seminal emissions can lead to problems with the heart and the kidneys and may be caused by distension of the bladder or rectum or pressure on the lower abdomen, but it may also be caused by psychic factors."

The quietness which accompanied Dr Hyde's examination and instructions was broken only by the sounds of stripping, rubber gloves, stainless steel, coughs, grunts, fountain pen on paper, and an occasional background car horn.

When they had resumed their seated interfacing postures, Dr Hyde informed Father Devine how he was concerned by the cracks and coating on Father Devine's tongue. Then, clearing his throat, he said, "You have an undescended left testis condition. Has that ever been looked at?" Blushing again, Father Devine outlined how his mother had vetoed an operation to have it brought down when he was an 11-year-old boy. Clearing his throat once more, Dr Hyde explained that due to the twenty-nine-year hiatus, there was a high risk of cancer having set in, and he would have to refer him to Sir Patrick Dun's Hospital for an operation to have the testis removed. Now believing Father Devine's "wet dreams" were most probably due to psychic reasons, Dr Hyde considered a placebo prescription pending surgery but settled on a high dosage of vitamin B complex in the hope of restoring some vigour.

That night, Dicey Riley did not come to Father Devine because sleep would not come to him. Instead, he was lost in boyhood embarrassments returned to haunt him.

Three men in white coats entered the classroom. Brother Colmcille ordered all students to line up around the classroom's walls and to drop their pants and underpants. The men in white coats then went on hunkers from pupil to pupil, feeling their scrotums and mandating coughs. Padhraig, the tallest of all the boys who always moved with an aura of divinity, suffered true humiliation when forced, pants around his ankles, to exit the classroom with a visible attack of diarrhoea. From his classmates' post-mortem on his "little mickey", Padhraig was reduced to a piteous slender streak of human misery despite his great devotion to St Patrick and his calling to the priesthood. Three months later, on National Health written instructions, Gabriel Devine's mother took him to a health clinic in Dublin city, where his scrotum and groin were examined, this time in the presence of his mother. A Dr deCantwell informed his mother an operation was needed to bring down his left testicle in advance of his attaining manhood. His mother demurred. Fuddled, Dr deCantwell prescribed daily groin-kneading techniques with an admonishment that should the testicle not drop within six months, an operation would be requisite.

At 3 a.m., the devil's hour, sleep still had not come, so Dicey Riley still had not come. Instead, Father Devine was consumed with fears of cancer.

His hospitalisation was traumatic, caused in part by sinister spinster Nurse Grainne, who tortured him with her sadistic grinning and suggestions how he might transmute into an androgynous devil or become another Hitler, who was also powered by only one ball—a half man, a half eunuch. Mortified into silence, Father Devine watched Nurse Grainne's large, sagging breasts as she clinically removed his pubic hair. She had drawn the curtains around his bed and matter-of-factly told him to remove his long johns because she had to get him nice and hairless for theatre, adding, "You don't want the young nurses shaving you down there, now, do you?" His capitulation remained nervous and nonverbal throughout the procedure. "There, there, you need fret no more. We're all done. Clean as a baby's bum," she said when finished, adding, "Turn yourself over now, and I'll slip this pellet up your back passage to make you nice and clean inside." Minutes later, Father Devine experienced the agony and the ecstasy of an explosive evacuation.

*Nurses Cara, Eithne, and Niamh appeared to him in green, white, and orange Druidic regalia, respectively. Nurse Niamh, holding a silver goblet in one hand and a phallic symbol in the other, moved closer and said, "This is a cup of meadowsweet and honey. You must drink it now and at every dusk hereafter till the next full moon." When he had drunk the contents from the goblet, Nurse Niamh, now stark naked, climbed onto his bed and sat astride him, straddling and clasping his phallus. Never before had he seen alive the milky white breasts or the pink paps of any fair maiden. Her areola and golden ringlets whirled, her blue eyes glistened, her nostrils flared, and her enticing lips opened and closed sporadically, moistened by the tip of her flickering tongue. Like a fairy goddess, she had mounted and consumed him until his mind was mindless, his body seedless and resting in the kingdom of bliss. Nurses Cara and Eithne then assisted a satiated Nurse Niamh from his bed and redraped her in her green hooded cape, covering her from forehead to toes. "Father Devine, how does it feel to have given your virginity to the princess of Tír ná nÓg?" asked Nurse Cara as all three departed into the abyss from whence they came.*

It was the morning after his operation when the buxom Nurse Eithne was attending Father Devine, and she became flabbergasted to find his scrotum was empty. Within minutes of her alarm, the surgeon, Dr O'Toole, and his entourage descended on the ward to investigate. "A right balls up," confirmed Dr O'Toole as he strode out of the ward, swearing. Following emergency counselling, Father Devine was returned to surgery to have his left undescended testis finally removed, and within twenty-four hours he was given the good and the bad news. It had not, as feared, become cancerous but useless by atrophy.

During his twelve days of convalescence and counselling in Sir Patrick Dunns, Father Devine was sanguine, cheerfully nursed by Nurses Cara, Eithne, and Niamh. Nurse Grainne, whom he suspected of a devilish role in his castration, had vanished.

An erudite solicitor visited to advise him of his right to claim damages. Father Devine would be able to bring a successful claim for negligence, which would be admitted. However, the core issue was quantum of damages. The solicitor posited, based upon his research, that there was an ineffable difference between the Western and Eastern practices of celibacy. In the East, it was esoterically cloaked in bandhas, mudras, mantras, and meditation. In the West, it was all about praying, pilgrimages, devotion, sex magic rituals, and cold baths. He submitted the raison d'être of Western celibacy derived from ancient shamanistic wisdom practices that were esoterically hermetically sealed, a mystery to be lived and not explained. Therefore, legal claims for loss of celibate practice would be problematic. He tried to end his submissions on a positive note and said, "At least you may be saved from the scourge of eczema, which in medieval times was believed to be caused by unfulfilled temptations of the celibate flesh." Father Devine then stipulated, not wanting to be exposed to legal or lifestyle philosophical value arguments, that he would accept a settlement that would cover his health care costs resulting from the hospital's gross negligence.

Alas, Father Devine finally forgave his beloved mother for denying him the operation when it might have been transformationally successful, because he now had personal experience why his mother feared operations as internal invasions that could kill but rarely cure. He could see her smiling down at him from heaven, imploring him to look on the bright side and continue his aspirations for a bishopric now twice freed from animalistic passion.

On departure day from Sir Patrick Dun's, Father Devine prayed he had been cured of his psychic problems. If not, he would rely upon the adulterous Dr Hyde for medicated help. Still, a voice from within hearkened from his seminal seminarian days. "Inri; ignis natura renovatur integra." "The fire renews nature incessantly." *Oh, well, he cajoled himself. In the absence of sublimation rights, there is always the last ecstatic sacrament, extreme unction.*

He gave his blessings to Nurses Niamh, Eithne, and Cara and stoically walked away.

# Mystique in Mustique

He was seated in the frog posture, staring out to sea or at the hummingbirds darting about, when I was escorted onto the veranda. Rising like a Greek god draped only in a Celtic cross and loincloth, he bid me, "Top of the morning," before adding, "I shall return anon."

I was conducting a soul-searching survey for the Mustique Company, the manager of Mustique Island. My methodology had been explained in a pre-survey pamphlet to each of its home owners. In a nutshell, I would meet one-on-one with the island's dons and divas and complete a checklist questionnaire of my educated guesstimates of their collective ratings. Each would then be invited to challenge those ratings in a confidential follow-up questionnaire and to state in one word or one sentence the ether of Mustique life.

He reappeared in a white crew T-shirt, navy Bermuda pants, and tan Sebagos, saying, "You know, you look just like the Mona

Lisa when you smile." I smiled, and he said, "The only problem is the Mona Lisa never smiles."

Staff at the Cotton House Hotel, where I had taken up residence for the duration of the survey, thought that Scobie Macan, nicknamed Lord Mac by the islanders, was a fugitive of sorts because he had not left Mustique since his arrival nine years ago, and unlike most of its non-belongers, he had no royal title. The cocktail crew at Basil's Bar said he was a mixture of a romantic, an eccentric, and a crook. However, I sat before him, in a rattan rocking chair, with an open mind. "Mr Macan," I started.

"Call me Scobie," he insisted. We were interrupted by the housekeeper placing a bottle of Hennessey XO and cognac glasses on the coffee table that separated us. "Help yourself," he said.

"I don't drink spirits before sundown," I replied.

"They keep me up," he jested. "If you don't mind, I take mine with a 100 per cent additive-free Nat Sherman. Better than snuffing it, though in days of yore, the aristocrats preferred it that way; apparently it gave them greater clarity and was said to be a powerful antidote for the dreaded headache."

I tried to start over and said, "Scobie, the dossier on this villa owned by the Viscountess of Fife records you as having a life interest and as being a naturalised citizen of St Vincent and the Grenadines."

"My mother, a lookalike for you," he replied, "was a great one for coining words. Perhaps it is not too late to have her honoured in the world of onomatopoeia." He then claimed his mother was prone to speak in tongues. When angry, her speech would be barbarous; when happy, she was a babbler. But no one, he lamented, had written down the magical words she'd uttered. Neither could he recall any to memory when I asked, and he expressed real shame at being unable to do so on the fiftieth anniversary of her passing.

While sitting on the palace's throne, I was confronted by a poster, a virginal-looking brunette holding a unicorn at her right side, a staff with a snake wrapped around it in her left hand. An unlikely source for a septuagenarian's daydreams, I imagined. He had a full head of white hair and all his teeth (except for his baby teeth, he had boasted), a perfect posture, and no pot belly. He also boasted he knew a little bit about everything and a whole lot about nothing. His only claim to fame that he volunteered was that he was the last of his mother's twelve children left on earth. He believed this placed an onus on him to do something, but what? That seemed to be his challenge—and apparently his agenda for my visit.

I returned to the veranda and tried to reset our meeting only to experience more deflection, including this riddle recording of what he said.

"Is the Holy Spirit the motive force for your Bostonian Harvard generation, or does it continue to be the avalanche from grace commenced by Adam and Eve? The cross of my daily cross is I grew up a heterogeneous child 'cause me mother and father were not me real parents."

He then related a story as it was told to him by Thelma—my lookalike, he said—who was not his biological mother but his earth mother. Thelma's eighth pregnancy had been a difficult one, and by the time she'd checked into the Rotunda to give birth, she was more dead than alive. After a long and painful labour, her baby was stillborn. During the night, when she was at her wits' end, Sr Angela visited her with a baby boy and asked if she would wish to take him home because his 16-year-old mother had abandoned him. And so Thelma had taken him home and treated him as her very own. When he was 16 and wanted to know more about the facts of life, that was what she had told him. It never mattered to him then or since, until presently when he realised he had not repaid her for all her loving-kindness. He now wanted to have Thelma dug up and given a proper Christian burial, but he didn't know where she was buried because she had simply disappeared, perhaps like him one fine day, without a trace.

He asked, "Have you ever met any shamans in your travels?" Not waiting for me to answer, he babbled on, perhaps like Thelma, about what he called a conspiracy of the hereafter. He said, "It may all be a load of exoteric codswallop and tommyrot," and he wouldn't waste more precious time hypothesising about it; his biological clock would reveal the truth soon enough because his biological mother had not only given him the miracle of birth but the mystery of death. "She must have been a very magical woman, like all women are," he said.

"Come," he said. "I have another picture of Athena in my bedroom to show you." On the wall facing his king bed was another poster. This one was a full-length nude of the woman in the guest loo. On the wall at the head of his bed was a Celtic cross. "So what do you think of my spiritual goddess? My mother had a great devotion to Athena and felt that because I should be a lifelong bachelor, I should adopt her to maintain me balance."

We moved on to the kitchen for coffee, and I was moved to ask, "Are you glad to have remained a lifelong bachelor?"

He said, "I'm glad I'm not sorry. Are you glad to be alone?"

I replied, "I suppose so."

"How do you look when you're sorry?" he teased. Then with tears in his eyes, he related how his only sweetheart had died of tuberculosis. "Before that tragedy," he whined, "her life was my life, her joy was my joy. On her deathbed, she was with child and wondered whether it would be delivered unto her in the next life."

While strolling back to the veranda, he said, "Sure, maybe Thelma didn't disappear at all. Come to think of it, maybe she ascended like the goddess. You know, Athena wasn't born naked like us—no, she appeared fully grown and half clothed out of her father's skull. But then, they say he was Zeus, a Greek god."

"So you're a Goodbye Johnny, Dear Irishman, Scobie Macan?"

"That I am, born and reared."

"So why Mustique?"

"Some soldiers of IRA destiny had to be disappeared for the making of the peace with Her Royal Highness, the Queen."

"And for that, the Viscountess of Fife allows you to live forever in her hiding palace and at her expense?"

He replied, "'Tis a spiritual pension I was granted for, as you should know. As you sow, so shall you reap."

I decided to discontinue the meeting given his belated frankness. On the way out, he revealed his only precondition for his exile was that his ashes would be returned to the Pucks Town Road as a last hurrah to his boyhood dreams. I noted a golf club standing alone in an umbrella stand at the front door. "You play golf too, Scobie?" I inquired.

He responded, "In my heyday, when I was at the height of me fame, that game was reserved for the gentry. So no, I have never played that game, but I learnt the pro, Lee Trevino, always carried a three iron during thunder and lightning because he maintained not even God could hit a three iron. So I carry one now on my evening walks."

I skipped lunch to walk on a sun-drenched beach and then lazed away the afternoon to consider the implications of Scobie Macan's revelations. He knew I was Boston Irish and Harvard educated, so what else would he know about me? That my mother and father, God rest their souls, had carried water for the cause? That I was an accredited member of the inner circle of the Daughters of Erin? That his secret was therefore safe with me? That I would think it sinister an IRA man could be given sanctuary a stone's throw away from a royal holiday home?

Back in my hotel suite following a long nap, I undressed to shower and found a rumpled sheet of paper in my blouse.

If you know Yeats,
You will know
Mustique is my Innisfree
and "Goodbye Johnny Dear".

PS Mahatma Gandhi took vows of celibacy and made the peace in the midst of a goddess.
PPS Ditto Tolstoy, who made *War and Peace.*

I now knew the bohemian Scobie Macan, or whoever he was, had had a hand in my blouse during our parting embrace.

In the shower, I found myself reciting, "I will arise and go now and go to Innisfree." But the rest of that Yeats's immortal poem would not come to me, though I repeated that line over and over until the water ran cold. I found a wellspring of peace within. I vowed to read "The Lake Isle of Innisfree" again, for the first time since sixth grade.

I was enjoying a predinner cocktail as the sun set over Basil's Bar when I spotted Scobie lilting along the seashore and swinging his three iron. I hurried down to engage him.

"'Tis not lake water, but 'tis lapping."

"Are you expecting a thunder and lightning storm tonight, to test that three iron?" I asked.

"No, but sometimes I think I could walk out into the Caribbean Sea to see how far I might get with it."

"You wouldn't be thinking of drowning yourself, now, would you?"

"As I can't swim, that would be a distinct possibility. So no, I'm not, because the ashes might not make it back."

"So you think you're Gandhi, Tolstoy, and Yeats all wrapped up in one?"

"Maybe not Yeats, because after his Golden Dawn years, he is reputed to have resorted to a vasectomy. But you, young lady, could be a vital final link to a Gandhi-like future for me."

That night, as a full moon enveloped Mustique, I believed that I became for him a reincarnation of Athena, until I flew with his ashes home and found my higher self.

# Kilcraic's Sixty-Three

After witnessing Simon's course record, I repaired with him to the clubhouse. There, over a few pints, I jotted down for posterity how it too had come to pass that day. It was, as Simon said, "not by happenstance but from true dedication to the game over umpteen years", and of course there was, as he admitted, "always lots of magic involved."

'Twas the morning after the night before, and Simon wasn't feeling himself that day, the day after his seventieth birthday party, so he decided to go outside to see if he was out there. In his backyard, he chastised himself, "Simon says he who stands up is not for lying down." With that reprimand, he gave himself an almighty slap on his backside to restart his inner man, just like the midwife might have done when he came out of paradise. He then went to the kitchen and took a shot of holy water. Feeling, as the scriptures had foretold, born again of water and the Holy Spirit, he returned to his bedroom and donned his favourite polo and slacks. With his game face on, he departed his home in his pride and joy, a BMW, bound for Kilcraic Golf Club with his Wilson Staffs and Footjoys in the boot.

Simon was indoctrinated in boyhood by Christian brothers in endless catechism classes of faith and riddles, one of which read, "Unless a man becomes like a little child, he shall not enter into the kingdom of heaven." The schoolyard banter wondered whether that process might be like growing up without growing old, sort of like how the old fogey of a school principal, Brother Fitzpatrick, had done. But with life's lessons learnt and an addiction to golf acquired, that not-so-idiotic-anymore riddle had for Simon matured into "To play or not to play—that is the question!"

As soon as Simon reached Kilcraic, he was struck by the heebie-jeebies when an inner voice told him, "Play as if these are your last eighteen holes." Without the luxury of a pro's pregame drilling routine and preparation time, he had for years followed the game plan enunciated by the mystical pro Shivas Irons in Michael Murphy's *Golf in the Kingdom*. To cut a legendary lesson short, in Simon's parlance, "Play every eighteen holes as three sixes: six holes to feel a centred swing, six holes to feel gravity, and six holes to score." Eerily, he feared if this was to be his last round, he may have innocently attracted the attention of that other mystical magus of three sixes fame, St Nicholas, aka the devil himself. Be that as it may, with jitters aside, Simon resolved to stick with Shivas Irons's three sixes game plan come hell or damnation.

Truth be told, Simon had long ago discovered Kilcraic was made for disciples of Shivas Irons, which was why he had become a member. The first six holes were laid out on flat lands, which aided a golfer's balance. The second six holes were all downhill, which reinforced a player's feel for true gravity. The final six holes comprised up-and-down rolling fairways, usually in crisscross winds. However, Simon always played them with Blarney lore, "with the wind always at me back and always scoring magical birdies or eagles, anything more being pure luck." So Simon said.

Shivas Irons had not appeared to 90 per cent of Kilcraic's members, and even if he had, they remained hackers. Many of them had quit ever trying to crack Hogan's secret. They suffered the consequences of poor grip, balance, tempo, or rhythm ailments, and they always shaved their scores with mulligans. They were, like me, invariably relieved to reach the clubhouse sober to enjoy a few pints. Of course, Simon, being a scratch player, enjoyed his after-game pints better than most. Fundamentally, he had the pro's Vardon grip, the balance of a ballerina, and a Sam Snead tempo to match. Like Bobby Jones, he took the club back with his right shoulder and so had a swing to die for. Though time and the tide had stolen some driving prowess, the seniors tee box, his shot-making skills, and his short game touch compensated for his ageing miseries. He had grown up to become a powerful competitor for Kilcraic on the senior amateur circuit.

That day, I had not been feeling meself either. Apart from Simon's birthday bash hangover, me sciatica was acting up again. I decided not to play but to walk along with Simon for the craic and to score and sign his card. As usual, he parred the first six holes in an exhibition of total relaxation with deadly aim. The next six holes of play appeared to be more of the same, except his forward swings were much more powerful and off much longer, lazy backswings. He had thee pars and three birdies. By the time we turned for home, he was in the golfer's zone, and with the wind at his back, he had no trouble at all sinking six more birdies for a nine-under-par round of sixty-three. When I told him that, he beamed his devilish grin and said, "Bejesus, Chivas, if that's to be me last round, I can live with that."

I said, "Jesus Christ, Simon, what's wrong with you? You just shot seven strokes below your age."

He said, "Sure, even that great Wilson Staff man Moses lamented that we might only get three score and ten in this kingdom of Golf."

Oh, and by the way, in case you're wondering, me nickname at Kilcraic is Chivas because I prefer that Scottish as a chaser.

> The game was invented a billion years ago—don't you remember?
> —Old Scottish golf saying

# The Kowtow

John (Jno.) Littlejohn, the prime minister's right-hand man, proposed the toast. "Here's to feasting on champagne and Peking duck soon." Dame Mary's kitchen cabinet trinity raised their glasses to her as if it were a fait accompli because the president was finally on his way for an unofficial visit to the People's Republic of China. "To be or not to be a banana republic" had been the fundamental question that had dogged her throughout her thirteen years as prime minister. The political mythomania demanded a paradigm shift via an international airport. Traditional partners couldn't or wouldn't help. Taiwan wouldn't help. That had left only China.

Peter Huang, charge d'affaires for the Republic of China on Taiwan in Lapsarianland, was crestfallen by the verbal communiqué. The prime minister's ultimatum was clear: either Taiwan funds an international airport, or diplomatic relations will be severed in favour of the One China policy. His instructions from Taipei were equally clear: continue his kowtow diplomatic service pending further instructions. He removed the black-and-white photograph of the president of Lapsarianland from its frame, threw it on the floor, and stomped on it.

The attorney general, flanked by two senior government ministers, arrived unannounced at the prime minister's home. Honourable Manners apologised profusely for the invasion of her privacy. "But," he said, "it is a matter of life and death because right-wing party members are up in arms."

The prime minister responded, "Remind them that ours is a political party, not a birthday party."

Honourable Pope was not amused by her recitation of that oft-repeated defence and asked, "Can the president be recalled, or is it too late?"

"He has landed in Beijing," the prime minister curtly stated.

The attorney general was aghast and blurted, "But Madam Prime Minister, where is the cabinet approval for all this?"

The prime minister eyed him steely, saying, "I have done the right thing in the right way for the right reasons."

The attorney general pressed his legal advantage. "But, Madam Prime Minister, that will not suffice."

Honourable Pope added, "And some party members want your head on a platter."

Honourable Manners then chimed in. "Please appreciate, Prime Minister, that Taiwan has, over all these years, treated our party members to great and honourable friendly relationships."

The prime minister gritted her teeth and asked, "Where is your testicular fortitude, gentlemen? Are you telling me if a proffer of an international airport is made by China, party members will not fall in line?"

Honourable Pope, breathing rapidly, replied, "What we came to tell you, Prime Minister, is that you must step down. Nothing else will pacify the parliamentary party rebels."

"In that event, gentlemen," replied the prime minister, "tell them I will complete my third term and then be gone."

Three days later, Ivo Tallyman, leader of the opposition, returned from an extemporaneous visit to New York elated. Now in front of his party national executive, he beamed. "A Taiwanese corporate consortium will fund the party's next general election campaign."

"Here, here," sang the chorus as their aggregate lust and greed for power consumed the meeting.

"In conclusion," Honourable Tallyman said, "ladies and gentlemen, with money now no longer our problem, I yield the floor as your honourable servant and your prime minister in waiting." The party spin doctor rose as the applause subsided to announce he could confirm there was incontrovertible evidence that the prime minister had conspired to bug their party headquarters and that an upstanding citizen would soon make a public confession to that effect, with the assurance of the fullest political opposition support in calling for the immediate resignation of the prime minister. This formalisation of the party's grapevine news was greeted with mixed, repeating shouts of "Madonna must go", "The virgin must go", and "The bugger must go."

When both were in state, the prime minister met with the president religiously every Wednesday at 9 a.m. for briefings on affairs of state. They broke with that ritual to meet the morning after the president's return from China. Intelligence sources reported the president would not be jet-lagged for the meeting but rather radiant. The prime minister thought so too when they shook hands.

"I've been to heaven, Mary. I'm ready to die."

"The sex was good, then, George?"

"I can assure you an international airport for Lapsarianland has been conceived."

The prime minister said, "The shame is I can't put it to the vote in cabinet because we will be blackballed."

"You must mothball it, then, and await the white smoke."

"Oh, don't be silly, George. The damned Freemasons are in revolt—they want my scalp."

"Madam Prime Minister, did you just call me silly? In that case, an apology would be in order."

"Don't you know, George? I would never call you silly, even if you were being silly."

The prime minister cut their meeting short on the pretext she had pressing state matters to attend to. She did not want to compromise the president further, given the political developments during his visit to China. On parting, the president undertook to submit a memorandum of his visit for the record.

James De Witt made his public confession on radio within hours of the president and prime minister meeting. He confessed to receipt of a caseload of cash from the prime minister with her verbal instructions to bug the opposition party headquarters. He named a government party operative as being present when he received his instructions from the prime minister. For days, De Witt's confession was all the talk shows talked about. The nation was divided as to whether De Witt was a halfwit or a cunning agent in a conspiracy to bring down the government. They also speculated whether the prime minister was capable of doing such a stupid Nixonian thing. Then the president acted to appoint a commission of inquiry.

Three days later, Honourable Christopher Reed was presumed dead, missing at sea. He had gone fishing, he had told party faithful, to clear his mind of the political shenanigans and to focus on his pledge to the prime minister to contest for the party leadership and to succeed her as prime minister.

"Jesus, Mary, and Joseph. Littlejohn, what the hell is going on in our little country?" the prime minister said.

"Tragic as it is, Prime Minister, we must circle the wagons and prevail somehow."

"It looks like this inquiry is going to be stalled indefinitely, what with all the foot dragging and posturing that's taking place."

"Fear no more, though, because you have the gumption to see the country through this grotesque, unprecedented debacle."

*One Year Later*

The day the Bahamian justice delivered his judgement, there were immediate statesman-like calls for the resignation of Ivo Tallyman. Judge Crossman's judgement was clear-cut: there was a book of no evidence to support the bugging allegations of James De Witt. Honourable Ivo Tallyman was roundly condemned, disgraced, and admonished for his unmitigated, egregious public support in the bugging charade.

Ivo Tallyman promptly called a press conference to fall on his sword in the hopes of saving his party, as advised by the party spin doctor. Eyeing the mutual admiration press corps from his pedestal, he announced his resignation as party leader and leader of the opposition forthwith. He would take no questions. "No more of that," he said. Instead, he offered the feeding frenzy a quote from Shakespeare's *Othello* as his political swan song.

> I pray you in your letters
> When you shall these unlucky deeds relate,
> Speak of me as I am, nothing extenuate
> Nor set down aught in malice.

An inept if not corrupt Lapsarian media granted Ivo Tallyman his political death wish, preferring instead to question the independence and bias of the sole judge commission of inquiry and the credibility of its findings of fact.

Ministers Manners and Pope arrived when summoned to the prime minister's office. "Thank you both for coming so promptly as requested," she said as they awkwardly seated themselves before her. "I will come straight to the point, gentlemen." She continued in the absence of any salutations being offered. "Hanzel, Alexander, thank you for your service to the state, but as you know, above all I value loyalty. When the chips were down, you gentlemen hid in the tall grass, so I want your resignations on my desk within the hour. Thank you, and God bless."

The prime minister's kitchen cabinet met several times that week to consider the omens for a snap election. By the weekend, they all saw nothing but a green light. The opposition party was in disarray, floundering to find a credible new leader; her nemeses, even if they ran as independents, would be defeated by the party's newly chosen candidates. Then she dropped her bombshell. "William Pitt from the youth wing will run and win my seat and replace me as prime minister."

Incredulously, Littlejohn responded, "Don't you think he is a mite young yet to take on that mantle?"

"He's the only one with the balls to do what we all agreed we must do," she responded.

"Alternatively," Littlejohn suggested, "you should stay on for a further term and transfer to him at a more appropriate time."

"I think not," she said. "I made my decision to go the night Manners and Pope came for my scalp. I'll not U-turn now. Besides which, I'm getting too old to endure any more political crap."

Immediately after being sworn into office as prime minister, William Pitt went directly to the Roman Catholic Cathedral to pray for guidance. From there, he went to Dame Mary's house to bid her bon voyage. She was in a headstand, being marvelled at by Littlejohn, when he entered her living room. She came out of her headstand to greet him warmly. "You will now find, Mr Prime Minister, that the art of successful politics is all about the ability to stand on one's head from time to time, so may I suggest you start practicing soon." He responded heartily and with his signature dimpled smile, which political pundits claimed had assured his landslide victory at the polls.

"The design plans for Virgil Pointe, courtesy of the UK's Iron Lady, are now with Littlejohn for when the Chinese team arrives."

"I shall propose to name this international airport Dame Mary in your honour."

"I think you should not do that, but for a project working title, the Great Houdini would be fitting."

"So noted. In any case, why have your name etched on a terminal building when it's already sealed in contemporary history and for posterity as the Great Madonna of the Caribbean?"

Her taxi arrived, and she left them to fetch her suitcase. Prime Minister Pitt looked at a sad Littlejohn and asked if he had any sage advice to offer. With raised eyebrows, Littlejohn replied, "Once upon a time, on an ambassadorial banana mission to Ireland, I learnt of a Celtic legend which tells that just three drops from the breast of a Black Madonna makes one spiritually invincible."

Once airborne, Dame Mary did not look down or back. She was free at last for a one-year sabbatical in Tibet. She believed that would be a gumption-free zone, at least.

# Golfer in the Rye

As a travel junky, I have rambled throughout an enchanting Dominica, the Nature Island of the Caribbean, an emerging remote and unique travel destination, the paradise home for a paradise lost Eden Resort. My walkabouts brought a telepathic connection with a fellow AD traveller, Evelyn Waugh, who was inspired by Dominica trails and wrote, "Sometimes it is enough to be beautiful. You don't have to bear fruit." A fitting accolade, I decided, whilst standing in the gloaming of the Eden Resort landscape, a triangle of true gravity.

Occasionally in recess from my roaming and journalising, I emailed Max, a fellow Irish émigré and a lifelong friend who has lived on Dominica's Godfull, golfless island this past forty years. His father had nicknamed him Max months before his phoenix birth, whilst watching Max Faulkner in the flesh sink his final putt to win the Open at Royal Portrush in 1951. His mentoring of young Max was undone by Christy O'Connor of Royal Dublin, who decreed Max didn't have the hands for a sustainable career as a professional golfer. Max came away from that gobsmack with the secret of the Vardon grip to fiddle with and a lament of how his bond with his dad was broken by "Christy's curse". His mother did not believe that was the case at all. She ranted about how Max's father got messed up from always sticking his nose in books he didn't belong in, like *Catcher in the Rye*. But there was no codding or cajoling Max as the key witness to his father's unmissable loss of interest in him.

I had planned to surprise Max, but when I arrived at his mountain cul-de-sac retreat, Eden Macha, it was deserted. Neighbours knew not of his whereabouts. One recalled last seeing him before Christmas with the villa's "mysterious caretaker". That was the season he turned 67. He had emailed me on his birthday, telling of how he stood "dormie three" and postulating about nearing three score and ten whilst entering a planetary age when the sun would be dimming and Mother Earth would encounter a mini ice age. It seemed to me, upon reading this stuff, that eccentricity was setting in. It would not be the first nor last time he spooked me. The last time he freaked out was following his fortieth birthday reading Michael Murphy's *Golf in the Kingdom*. As it turned out, he later wrote he had had a premonition and bolted to Scotland to discover the spirit of Shivas Irons, the inspirational professional golfer of Michael Murphy's ken yoga journeys. On his return, Max related he had indeed discovered the spirit of Shivas Irons on every Scottish golf course he played because he had played them for the thrills of the walkin' and not the ecstasy of the shots or the scores. After his Scottish sojourn, he reverted to haunting the golf courses of the Caribbean, from Mount Irvine in the south to Caymanas in the north, to maintain his balance. It was a balance that he sensed arose on the road hole of St Andrews, which inspired him to name his villa Eden Macha, in remembrance of Dominica's Eden daydreams and our boyhood scouting days at Emhain Macha, the ancient royal capital of Celtic Ireland and the eternal pursuits of the goddess Macha.

I was finalising plans for my trek to the boiling lake one of Dominica's beckoning natural wonders when Max finally replied to my SOS.

> I'm rambling on the auld sod and haven't had email access till now. This getaway having been declined a reverse mortgage on Eden Macha to mount a Mt Everest expedition for me sixty-eighth birthday. When the medical report came back, it put my bio age at 51, so my bookie wouldn't take the risk of me not dying in short order. Of course, this means I shall be dormie eighteen come November. I have woken up without even going to sleep—kinda like being born again. So far I've had great indulgences all over Armagh and Emhain Macha, and I'm now proceeding to visit all the other sacred sites of Eire. Kinda like a pilgrim's journey around the island of saints and scholars. With a bit of luck and the road rising to meet me, I shall reach Royal Portrush in July and relish the Open outside the ropes, as me father before did. The keys to Eden Macha are with Dion Fortune @ 616-7777. Make yourself at home.

Having led a wandering, Hibernian lifestyle since my parents had clocked out in 1977, I thought I had met all shades of romantics, eccentrics, and crooks, but I was mistaken. Dion Fortune introduced herself to me as a reincarnated Welsh occultist who'd died on 8 January 1946 in London, England. Dominican born and reared, and known as Shauna McDuff, she was Dion Fortune, an awakened Taoist sage to her hermetic K Club members. Overtly, she was a 73-year-old naturalist and yoga instructor by day. Covertly by night, she was an ageless ceremonial magician in the astral plain. She arrived at Papillote Wilderness Retreat in a flaming yellow Land Rover as I was checking out, exactly three hours after I had phoned her—as she predicted she would. One hour later, having listened mesmerised to her musings, I was planted in Eden Macha with a complimentary copy of her 1938 novel, *The Sea Priestess*, and a kitchen stocked with local foods until I would need to go venture shopping in Roseau. She told me I looked the worst for the wear of my 68 years, that I was going to seed, and that my balls were low! Naturally, before my rising protestations erupted, she offered post-haste to work wonders for me, as she had for Max since his fiftieth birthday. Therefore, in parting, I felt bunkered to await her return on Sunday at 5 a.m. for an introductory yoga lesson.

Externally, Eden Macha had an aura of a joint Celtic cross standing beneath a halo of dove-white sky in reverent embrace of its panoramic view of luminous blue seascape and verdant mountains. Internally, its feng shui exuded the atmospherics of a Celtic temple for convoking a peaceful and solemn gathering of mindfulness. Those were my gleanings as I lay in corpse posture on its secluded, eastern-facing greenheart veranda, nursing my weary body from the afterglow of hiking across the Valley of Desolation, crowned off by the elation of the boiling lake summit.

She arrived at 4.55 a.m. and rearranged me into Sukhasana, a so-called easy sitting posture, to watch her disrobe to a one-piece yellow swimsuit and perform the five Tibetan rites. To my spellbound eyes, she did so as an 18-year-old ceili dancer would. Then she indoctrinated me into each rite with a strict ten-week performance programme, at the end of which she promised I should be ripe to find my inner man again. She departed at sun up to the sound of distant bagpipes of her Scottish ancestry humming in my ears.

Following five weeks of 5 a.m. performances of the five

Tibetan rites, I was anxious for a eureka comparable to my rivers, falls, lakes, and emerald pool penetrations of Dominica's enticing natural splendours. Instead, I had to chew over another intriguing email from Max.

I've been to countless sacred Celtic pagan and Christian sites and am delirious to believe they exist to herald a renaissance of the Celtic Christian way. These are the sacred sites of St Bridgid, St Patrick, and St Malachy to name only a famous threesome. But I must also mention St Ciaran's holy well, at which his bell rang out to me to heed his cry. And I did. Outside these hallowed, downtrodden sacred sites, the Roman Catholic Church has fallen from grace, hoisted by its own inverted mortal sins as was the Roman Empire before it. No wonder, then, the archbishop of Dublin from his pro-cathedral pulpit has wailed for the mass media to expose how violence in the capital has taken on an unprecedented level of depravity. I am now a witness to the Celtic Tiger, having been slain by the machinations of Europe's Fourth Reich. Pride, covetousness, lust, anger, gluttony, envy, and sloth—the seven deadly sins are rampant throughout the length and breadth of the land. Belongers are bawling about their cultural internment by a mass influx of carpetbaggers. There is weeping and gnashing of teeth amongst her awakened, her mist-walking sons and daughters. After more than one hundred years of independence, lyrics of "A Nation Once Again" are being sung in every nook and cranny. A landslide of patriot ballots is being canvassed by Brian Boru spiritual warrior clans. The proclamation of the 1916 Easter Rising has replaced the "above" and "below" underground secrets of the green tablet. The souls of Kilmainham Gaol's liberty martyrs are still at large from dusk to dawn and must be freed. I tarry now along the Wild Atlantic Way to recharge my batteries—to allow my soul catch up with my body, so to speak.

The plight of the Irish was driven home to me whilst hill walking in the Kalinago Territory, the pristine reserve of the indigenous people of Dominica. If Cromwell had had his "to hell or to Connacht" way, the Irish homeland would have become the wondrous bogs of Connemara. The Great Irish Famine collusion was also thwarted as a final solution to the Irish question. So Ireland was morphed into an EU colony, spawning the Irish downfall to minoritarians in their reengineered ancestral homeland.

On the eve of the Open, Max emailed from his "lovely bed and breakfast digs run by a gorgeous landlady on the outskirts of Portrush."

For the next four days, I will be on the course to golf without golfing. 'Tis a triangle of giant sandhills, emerald turf, and a tarot deck of eighteen holes with macabre legends to rival the Bermuda Triangle. Perhaps I shall seance with Shivas on White Rocks (the fifth hole) or with me dad in Purgatory (the seventeenth hole). The locals boast it was created "as a monument more enduring than brass." It is protected by giants of the Giants Causeway and the banshees of Dunluce Castle. So there is all to play for! If spared, on Monday I depart to a Celtic Christian retreat on the Aran Islands, where we will consult the Celtic Runes at the medieval ruins of the Seven Churches. Thereafter, I march to the drums of Celtic Christian Revivalists.

Dion sat in lotus. I lay in a spirit of longing, in corpse pose. It was countless minutes since our five rites 5 a.m. ritual when her spell unbounded. "Listen a while to me, Seamus." Her voice sounded hypnotic.

*Perhaps it's her sea priestess mode,* I thought.

She continued. "After ten weeks of transformation by the five Tibetan rites, you walk tall with a glint in your eyes. Your gait is that of a young man. Your paunch has receded. Your eliminations have become effortless. You may even feel full of spit and vinegar!" I grinned as she continued. "I now offer you passage to the next level to discover the mysteries of Kriya Yoga, which transcends the joyful, sorrowful, and glorious mysteries of your Catholic rosary. A forty-day and forty-night quest awaits at my beehive rainforest cell. A quest to confront life's three choices: to generate, to degenerate, to regenerate. I will school you in the ancient art of Kriya. Thereafter, if practiced faithfully with the five Tibetan rites, you will attain true enlightenment. You will discover the bliss of heaven on earth, your so-called Holy Grail."

Following a long interlude of simmering silence, I was thrust into lotus and declared my epiphany. "Once upon a time, it was chronicled how the Irish saved European civilisation. Now the Irish must save Irish civilisation. I shall now be about my forefathers business because that is the Celtic Christian way of the Irish."

She responded in the way of her Taoist master. "Lao Tzu says, 'Cultivate the self, and the action is pure. Cultivate the family, and the action is plentiful. Cultivate the community, and the action endures. Cultivate the nation and the action is fruitful. Cultivate the world, and the action is all-pervading.'"

# Epilogue

## Betwixt and Between

At Newgrange in Ireland, there is a tomb that was built five thousand years ago. Every dawn on the morning of the winter solstice (21 December), the main chamber is illuminated by a beam of sunlight for seventeen minutes. It is believed this tomb is the oldest surviving so aligned structure in the world. When I visited this time capsule in 2010, I was reading Osho, named by the *Sunday Times* of London as one of "the most dangerous men since Jesus Christ" because he preached the power of the individual as a rebel—that human culture was nothing more or less than striving to lead the ordinary life in an extraordinary way. Providentially, my Newgrange tomb and otherworld arousal snatched my soul's return to the Celtic way.

Percy Bysshe Shelley, confronted by elusive pursuits of balance in his life, concluded his immortal sonnet, "I balanced all, brought all to mind, the years to come seemed waste of breath, a waste of breath the years behind, in balance with this life, this death." Carl Jung challenges a Shelley-like conundrum with his philosophical dictum: "Who looks outside dreams; who looks inside awakens." In Thomas Cahill's *How the Irish Saved Civilisation*, readers are put on notice: the twenty-first century will be spiritual, or it will not be.

Subliminal meditation on such Roman Catholic heresies did not still the tug of the past or the tug of the future within. Revisiting William Butler Yeats, a leader of the twentieth-century Irish Nationalist Movement and Ireland's greatest poet, did. I was kindled to journey on *Celtic Irish Arousals* by his daunting, inciteful poetry.

> When Pearse summoned Cuchulan to his side,
> What stalked through the Post Office? What intellect,
> What calculation, number, measurement, replied?
> We Irish, born into that ancient sect
> But thrown upon this filthy modern tide
> And by its formless spawning fury wrecked,
> Climb to our proper dark, that we may trace
> The lineaments of a plummet-measured face.
> —William Butler Yeats, "The Statues"

Yeats was also a leading light of the Irish Literary Revival (nicknamed the Celtic Twilight) of the nineteenth and twentieth centuries. In his Celtic Twilight short stories, he bemoaned Celtic Ireland was being lost. Moreover, his Irish Nationalist Movement stands jilted at the altar of European integration. I pray this interregnum may be redressed in times to come.

Meanwhile,
May *Celtic Irish Arousals* provide some succour to seekers and readers alike.

May it nourish minds, hearts, and spirits.
And until we may meet again,
May the life, the light, and the way be with you.

Kieron Pinard-Byrne
September 2019

Printed in the United States
By Bookmasters